HDS

St. Helens Libraries

Please return / renew this item by the last date shown.
Books may be renewed by phone and Internet.

Telephone - (01744) 676954 or 677822
Email - centrallibrary@s
Online - sthelens.gov.uk
Twitter - twitter.com/STH

KU-545-083

C21 -- DEC 2016	G18 -- APR 2022
K11 -- MAR 2017	D9 -- AUG 2023
M3 -- SEP 2017	
Q14 - APR 2018	
M3 -- AUG 2017	
Q8 -- OCT 2018	
C21 -- FEB 2019	
J16 -- JAN 2020	
-1 JUL 2021	
DK -- AUG 2021	

THE FAMILY AT CLOCKMAKERS COTTAGE

Feeling bereft after her sister Fanny gets married and moves away, young Amy Macfarlene must manage Clockmakers Cottage on her own, while earning a living as a parlour maid and seamstress for a wealthy local family, the Paslews. Her wayward brother Rory is a constant concern, as he is clearly embroiled in some shady dealings and refuses all offers of help. Amy's childhood sweetheart Dan is a comfort to her — but as her friendship with the handsome Gilbert Paslew grows, so do her uncertainties about her future . . .

Books by June Davies
in the Linford Romance Library:

IN DESTINY'S WAKE
THE APOTHECARY'S DAUGHTER
THE FAMILY BY THE SHORE
THE FIDDLER'S WALTZ

JUNE DAVIES

THE FAMILY AT CLOCKMAKERS COTTAGE

Complete and Unabridged

LINFORD
Leicester

First published in Great Britain in 2008

First Linford Edition
published 2016

A catalogue record for this book is available
from the British Library.

ISBN 978–1–4448–3054–5

Published by
F. A. Thorpe (Publishing)
Anstey, Leicestershire

Set by Words & Graphics Ltd.
Anstey, Leicestershire
Printed and bound in Great Britain by
T. J. International Ltd., Padstow, Cornwall

This book is printed on acid-free paper

1

Amy Macfarlene lay wide awake, brooding upon the bitter argument she'd overheard between Fanny's betrothed and his younger brother. Staring up at the low beams crossing the ceiling of the long room under the eaves of Clockmakers Cottage, she expelled a weary breath. Although exhausted after her long day's work at Whiteladies Grange, sleep would not come. Theodore and Nicholas Buxton's angry words persisted in churning around her mind, planting seeds of doubt about the man her elder sister was about to marry.

Restless, Amy turned to gaze out at the sky. It wouldn't be daylight for hours yet. The tide was far out, she knew, yet its soft rush and whisper drifted across the still night air to creep through the open windows and fill the silent stone cottage overlooking the bay at Monks Quay.

Both of Amy's sisters were sleeping soundly, and she shifted slightly in the old high bed to be more comfortable, mindful of not disturbing Fanny, who was lying next to her like a sleeping princess. Extract of eyebright soaked the muslin pads upon her closed eyes, and her shining fair hair was neatly coiled into curl-rags. Fanny wanted to look her best for her wedding day.

Amy frowned. Truth to tell, hadn't she always felt a little uneasy about Fanny's whirlwind romance with Theodore Buxton? She had never quite trusted him, somehow. Theo was just too good to be true. Too handsome. Too charming. Too perfect. Or were her misgivings, Amy considered in her honest fashion, simply because Theo unsettled her? He was a stranger, completely different from anyone she'd ever met, and from a sophisticated world far removed from the one the Macfarlenes belonged to in Monks Quay. Nonetheless, should she have told Fanny, warned her, and related everything she'd overheard the previous evening up at Whiteladies Grange?

It had been during the customary lull before the Paslews and their guests went down to dinner in the panelled refectory, which in olden times had been part of the abbess's lodgings. Having carried a basket of laundered and pressed linen up to the warming cupboard, Amy was taking fresh towels into each room. She was just finishing in Gilbert Paslew's corner dressing-room, remembering to leave a new tablet of the sandalwood soap Mr Gilbert favoured next to his pitcher and basin, and was about to slip through the adjoining door into the guest room when she heard Theodore Buxton's voice, and ducked back. It was probably foolish, but Amy felt uncomfortable and tongue-tied whenever she bumped into her future brothers-in-law here at Whiteladies — where she was a parlour maid, and they guests of her master.

Already deep in heated conversation, the Buxton brothers entered the guest room, and Amy was taken aback at the agitation in Nicholas's quiet voice.

'It's no use, Theo!' he was saying. 'You shan't talk me round to your way this time. I can't imagine why I ever let you persuade me to go along with it in the first place.'

'Because, dear boy, you know this is the perfect scheme,' Theodore Buxton returned carelessly, lighting a cigarette. 'Besides, what options have we? A first son inherits the family pile and the second goes into the army. Well, the least said about the Buxton family pile the better, and you haven't the slightest aptitude for going to some far-flung corner of the empire and subduing the natives. You just don't have the stomach for a fight, Nick.'

'I don't have the stomach for this . . . this *deception*, either!'

'May I remind you who it was that brought me to Whiteladies last summer to visit your old school chum?' snapped Theodore. 'You made the introductions, and I simply made the best use of them. Is it my fault old Paslew's greed knows no bounds? He almost tore my arm off when I mentioned those shares.'

'Yes, but — '

'But nothing,' cut in Theodore, pouring himself a whiskey. 'You knew my motives for coming to Whiteladies, although even I could not have anticipated the astounding success of the venture. Paslew is like all men of his sort. However much money and power they acquire, it's never quite enough.'

'It's not Alfred Paslew and his wretched money I'm worried about — well, not entirely, anyhow. He's a businessman. A speculator. And pretty ruthless too, by all accounts,' pressed Nicholas. 'It's Fanny and the Macfarlenes I'm concerned about.'

'What about them?'

'It's gone far enough, Theo!' responded Nicholas fervently, and from the gap in the doorway, Amy could see how pale and disconcerted he looked. 'You should tell Fanny the truth.'

Theodore's pleasing countenance was suddenly sly. 'Taken a shine to the girl yourself, have you? Can't say I'm surprised. Fanny does have the face of an angel. And such dainty, vain manners, despite hailing from a cultural desert like Monks Quay. She's a spirited filly, too. I couldn't have chosen better.'

'Then be honest with her,' demanded Nicholas. 'For God's sake, Theo, you're getting married in a couple of days, and Fanny has all those false impressions you've given her.'

'Calm down, for goodness sake. What have I done to Fanny or her family that is so unconscionably dreadful? I proposed to the girl!' he exclaimed, sitting in one of the winged chairs at the side of the fireplace. 'Fanny Macfarlene wants a husband, and to escape from this godforsaken speck on the map. And I need an attractive wife who looks and behaves like a lady, yet whose family are simple folk who don't ask too many questions. We both of us are getting what we want. What's so wrong about that? Anyway, Fanny loves me and I absolutely adore her. You're not about to spoil true love, are you?'

'Surely love depends upon honesty and trust.' Nicholas turned away from his brother, gazing out across the gardens of Whiteladies to the distant hills. 'You're deceiving Fanny, and it's wrong.'

'You can't jeopardise my marriage to Fanny without ruining my enterprise with Alfred Paslew,' remarked Theodore evenly. 'I'm not about to let that happen, Nick. I won't allow you to lose your nerve now.'

'I should've spoken out sooner,' the younger man muttered wretchedly.

'Take my advice, as you always have,' Theodore replied easily, his smile even and white. 'Let me do all the thinking. Be my best man in every respect and we'll all live happily ever after!'

Amy had shuddered as she watched and listened from the adjoining room. Despite the smoothness of his manner, there was undeniable menace behind Theodore's words. He rose, pushing his brother towards the door. 'Go to your room and I'll see you at dinner. If you

7

fancy a little sport afterwards, I'm going to the Mermaid for a few hands of cards. Monks Quay may be a desolate hole, but there's considerable wealth amongst the merchant classes in these little market towns.' His full mouth curved. 'I wager I'll soon hear the jingle of their purses.'

Nicholas quit the room and the oak door closed. Theodore turned towards the dresser, pouring himself another drink. Amy waited a moment or two, ensuring the landing was clear before slipping from Gilbert Paslew's dressing-room. Theodore Buxton's fresh towels were still in her arms and for that instant quite forgotten, as with a pounding heart she scurried along the landing to the backstairs and fled to the safety of the kitchen.

Now, in the stillness of the early summer's night, Amy rubbed her throbbing temples with her fingertips. Slipping from the big bed, she moved across to the window and breathed deeply the cool, clear sea air. Sitting on the oak chest, she tucked her knees beneath her chin and stared out into the darkness. Pa was out there somewhere, making the homeward crossing, likely going in to port at Liverpool before sailing the final miles up to Monks Quay.

For a long while after Ma died, the cottage had seemed unbearably empty whenever Pa was away on the packet. But without even realising it, Amy had grown accustomed to managing the household with Fanny. She did not count Rory. Despite being five years Amy's senior, her brother was irresponsible and unreliable. Even Fanny's sharp tongue was becoming less and less effective at curbing Rory's sullen wildness. In just a few days, Amy would have to cope with everything on her own. The prospect weighed heavily. She lacked Fanny's brisk manner and self-assurance, but from now on Vicky and Edmund — and Pa, too — would be depending upon her.

A chill breeze crept up from the beach, and Amy rose to fetch her shawl. The uneven floorboard creaked beneath her bare foot as she reached up to the hook beside Vicky's bed, and the child stirred.

'Is Pa home yet?'

'Shhh, it's still night,' whispered Amy, smoothing a stray strand of hair from her sister's forehead. 'Go back to sleep.'

'Will Pa be able to see his way home?' Vicky yawned, rubbing her eye with her fist. 'Is the Dog Star shining?'

'It's shining brighter than all the other stars, just like always,' Amy reassured Vicky, as her heavy eyelids fluttered closed. 'Lighting up the sea so Pa can sail straight home to us.'

Straightening up, Amy tiptoed from the bed, carefully avoiding the creaky floorboard.

'There's no need to creep!' Fanny's voice was crisp.

'Thought you were asleep, Fan.'

'I was,' returned Fanny, removing the muslin pads from her eyes before sitting up and pounding the pillows into a comfortable mound. 'I certainly hope —'

'Shh,' interrupted Amy, climbing back into bed. 'Vicky's gone off to sleep again.'

'I certainly hope Pa gets home promptly,' Fanny said in a low voice. 'He was almost a week late coming back from his last trip.'

'That wasn't Pa's fault. There was some problem with the *Jenet Rae*, you know that.'

'I also know I need a father to give me away.'

'I'm sure Pa will be back, Fan. But you never can predict the weather and the seas.'

'Pa is skippering a packet up and down the coast and back and forth to the Isle of Man and Ireland, not voyaging to the Americas,' retorted Fanny crossly, fussing with her ringlets. 'However, it is exactly as you have it — one can never be certain of weather or seas. I only wish Pa hadn't sailed so close to my wedding day.'

'He can't refuse to sail, Fan,' protested Amy mildly, aware her sister was anxious the wedding be perfect. 'Pa

11

couldn't afford to lose his wages for the trip. Besides, Mr Paslew would probably have sacked him if he'd refused the ticket.'

'That wretched boat would make better time if Alfred Paslew would get it shipshape,' went on Fanny, hitting her stride now. 'I know for a fact Pa's told him what needs doing on the *Jenet Rae*. Paslew's willing enough to make profit from the packet, but he won't spend an extra shilling on her! It's not as though he can't afford it,' she commented tartly. 'Paslew's the richest man in Monks Quay, and getting richer by the year. Mrs Ainsworth was telling me she heard he's recently taken over the brick kilns at Hawridge and opened up an office in Lancaster.'

Amy drew breath to speak, then bit her tongue. How had Theodore described Alfred Paslew? A man whose greed knew no bounds? She hardly ever saw her master while working at Whiteladies Grange, but was well aware Paslew had the reputation of being shrewd in business and dangerous to cross.

'When Pa gets back,' she reflected at length, 'it'll be the last day the family will be together, won't it?'

'I hadn't thought about it, but yes.' Fanny exhaled a slow, contented breath. 'My last days as Miss Fanny Macfarlene. Oh, I can't wait to be married, Amy! To finally be swept away from this suffocating little town and have a fine home of my own. Theo has told me so much about his house in Carteret Square, I feel as though I know every room already. And York is such a splendid city, I'm told. We'll entertain, have dinner parties, attend concerts and the theatre. I shall shop at only the finest establishments and wear beautiful clothes.' She turned to Amy, her pretty face animated and her blue eyes sparkling. 'Theo and I are going to have such a wonderful life. Everything I've ever dreamed of.'

'I couldn't bear to go away,' commented Amy softly. 'Won't you be even a little homesick?'

'I shall miss you and Pa and the children. I'll even miss Aunt Anne, despite her constant fussing and disapproval of everything. However, I'll scarcely miss Rory at all! He's always been surly and hot-headed, but he's grown worse of late. I fear he's fallen in with a rough crowd at the clay pits, Amy. You'll need to be careful, or Rory will walk all over you. When Pa's away, our brother has taken it into his head he can do whatever he pleases. He can't, and you mustn't allow him to take advantage.' Her smooth brow creased. 'Unless he mends his ways, Rory will come to a very bad end indeed.'

Amy had scarcely been listening, her thoughts preoccupied with Fanny's rosy anticipation of her marriage. 'Fan, how can you be — I mean, are you sure Theo is right for you? After all, barely a year ago you'd never even met. You haven't actually spent much time together, have you?' she blurted hurriedly. 'We don't know much about him or his family, do we? How can you be sure Theo's the man you want to spend the rest of your life with?'

'I knew Theo was the man for me from the moment we were introduced at that dreadful church social.' Fanny smiled, her eyes soft. 'And I've thanked my lucky stars every day since! I'm nearly twenty-three, Amy. I'd virtually given up hope of ever marrying and I was scared of being alone like Aunt Anne. At least she has her school, but without marriage, what would I have had? Whatever would have become of me?'

Amy was shocked. 'How could you ever have thought that way? You're beautiful, Fan! You could have had lots of suitors, if only you'd let them come calling!'

'Fishermen, plough-boys and shop-keepers. Dull as ditchwater and utterly lacking in ambition.' She shook her head in exasperation, adding gently, 'You're like Ma, Amy! It means something to you that Ma's family lived here for generations. You love Clockmakers Cottage

15

and the shore and the sea and Monks Quay, but I don't. I've always felt so . . . so trapped! When Theo proposed, it was like being set free, and suddenly I knew I didn't need to worry anymore and everything was going to be all right. You're still very young, Amy. You might not understand.'

'I do! I do, really,' Amy replied hastily. 'It's just . . . When I was at Whiteladies last evening, I overheard Theo and Nicholas talking. Well, arguing, I suppose. Nicholas was saying . . . It sounded as though . . . That is, I don't think Theo has been honest with you, Fan, and — '

'Amy, that's quite enough!' interrupted Fanny sharply. 'You should not have been eavesdropping, and whatever you imagine you heard could not be of less interest to me. I believe I know my future husband rather better than you do, and I trust Theo completely. He's a perfect gentleman. I'm deeply hurt you should suggest such otherwise.'

'Fanny, I'm so sorry. I didn't want to

upset you. I only thought — '

'Theo and I are to be married, Amy,' cut in Fanny. Reaching for the muslin pads, she lay down and covered her eyes once more. 'Please try to be happy for me.'

'I am . . . ' said Amy, her voice trailing to silence. It was still very early, but far too agitated to rest, she rose and slowly began dressing.

* * *

Padding in her stockinged feet along the landing past their parents' empty room and the smaller one next to it where her two brothers slept, Amy moved swiftly through the darkness and down the steep, crooked staircase into the stone-flagged kitchen. As soon as she lit the lamp, she saw that the cold supper of bread, cheese and pickled onions Fanny had left for Rory had remained untouched on the sideboard.

Getting to her knees, Amy began raking out the warm ashes and setting the fire, frowning thoughtfully while she worked. When she had arrived home from Whiteladies last evening, Rory had already been in from the clay pits and, according to Fanny, gone straight out again without eating his meal; hence the cold supper. Where could he have been headed in such a rush? The Green Man probably, Amy reasoned dismally. The Green Man was a rough tavern on the outskirts of Monks Quay and much frequented by the clay-pit men.

It was possible Rory had come home so late that he'd gone up to bed without eating anything, but glance to the back of the door, where Rory's coat was missing, proved that wasn't so. He'd never stayed out the whole night before. Wafting the fire gently into life so it wouldn't smoke, Amy put together the makings of breakfast before starting upstairs again.

Pushing open the door of her brothers' room, she could make out the lighter shape of Rory's narrow bed, which was flat and unoccupied.

'Amy? Is that you?' Edmund's voice was low. 'I've been awake ages. Where's Rory? He hasn't been in all night.'

'I know, Teddy,' she replied. 'Did he say anything when he got home from the clay pits last night? Where he was going? What he was doing?'

Edmund grinned. 'Rory doesn't tell me anything.'

Amy nodded. There were almost seven years separating the brothers, and about all they had in common was their family name. 'I've lit the fire and started breakfast, but it's far too early to serve it up.' She glanced through the small-paned window to the sky before turning from the room. 'Rory's due at the clay pits in a couple of hours or so. He'll be put on notice if he's late.'

Following her downstairs, Edmund hesitated before speaking. 'He'll be sacked, Amy. Charlie Thorpe at school, whose brother works at the clay pits, told me that old Bostock the overseer put Rory on notice a couple of weeks ago for talking back. Charlie said

Bostock is a right old bug, is really strict, and Rory was lucky not to be sacked on the spot.'

'Teddy! Why didn't you tell Fanny and me about this?'

Edmund shrugged uncomfortably. 'I couldn't, Amy! I couldn't tell tales. Where are you going?'

'To find Rory. If he loses his job, word will get around he's unreliable, and no one else will take him on.'

'I'll come with you.'

'No, stay here. I'll be fine, Teddy. I'll take the light.'

Touching a flame to the lantern, Amy let herself out into the chill, dark morning. Her footsteps were silenced by the coarse sand as, swinging the lantern from side to side and casting its beam wide lest Rory had passed out in his cups on the track leading home, she swiftly left Clockmakers Cottage behind and started the steep walk up towards the town.

The rough track presently became cobbles and soon Amy passed by Aunt

Anne's schoolhouse, continuing on around All Hallows into the market square. Pausing at the ancient village cross, Amy's gaze swept the dark streets and buildings, trying to penetrate the great wells of blackness yawning away beyond every archway, ginnel and narrow twisting lane. Rory might be anywhere! Here, in the deserted town. Down by the quayside. Up in the hills, where the scars of Paslew's workings showed pale. He could be lying amongst the dunes, or on the shore. Perhaps he'd stayed the night with a workmate in one of the ramshackle terraces of mean dwellings the clay pits and quarry had spawned. If that were so, she'd never find him!

Hopeless as it seemed, Amy raised the lantern once more and, looking in doorways and along alleys as she went, began walking. She started onto the town's main thoroughfare, and had gone just a few hundred yards along Abbotsgate when the glowing lights of the Mermaid came into sight and she heard the whicker and stamp of horses as she approached the coaching inn's neat yard. Brisk footsteps were ringing on the cobbles, and Amy jumped when a low voice hailed her from the shadows.

'Amy? Amy Macfarlene?' The footsteps quickened and a broad-shouldered figure strode from the Mermaid's yard within the beam of her lantern. 'Good God, whatever are you doing in town at this hour? Is owt wrong? Is it the packet?'

'No, Dan. Nothing like that. Pa's not due back till this evening. It's . . . ' She faltered, reluctant to speak of family troubles even with somebody she'd known since her school days. 'It's Rory. He didn't come home last night.'

'Your brother's a grown man,' returned Dan Ainsworth stiffly, shifting the weight of the harness slung across his shoulder. 'You shouldn't be out in the pitch dark looking for him.'

'I think he might've gone to the Green Man. He probably got drunk,' she mumbled, shamefaced. 'He'll lose his job if he doesn't turn up to the clay pits on time.'

'I'll help you look.'

'I can manage, Dan!' she cut in. 'You have work to do. You've to be ready for the first coach.'

'There's time enough yet. And even if there weren't, I'd not let you go wandering around Monks Quay searching for a drunkard.' Dan turned on his heel towards the stables. 'Let me fetch a light and we'll be on our way. Don't fret, lass,' he added over his shoulder. 'Rory's got sharp wits and a hard head. He'll not have come to any great harm.'

All Hallows clock was striking the quarter-hour as they proceeded along Abbotsgate in the general direction of the Green Man, with Amy keeping a sharp lookout to one side and Dan to the opposite. Their footsteps were loud upon the steep street and seemed the only sounds in the whole town.

'This is kind of you, Dan,' she murmured at length. 'I appreciate it more than you know. Rory's got into bad company at the clay pits.'

'Don't make excuses for him! It's a

disgrace, him carrying on like he does,' said Dan tersely. 'Rory should be taking care of his family when your da is away, not having his sister running herself ragged because he can't hold his ale.'

'I know you're right,' Amy said at length. 'Rory seems only to care for himself, but I do worry about him. I can't help it.'

'Aye, you always were the soft-hearted one. Even as a little lass.' He smiled across at her, adding with a frown, 'I reckon you may have cause to be concerned, Amy.'

'What's happened?' she demanded, the knot of anxiety tightening within her.

'Maybe nothing.' He shrugged. 'I don't know anything for sure.'

'You live in town, Dan; you know what's going on. At the Mermaid, you're bound to see things. Hear things.' She spoke rapidly, turning to him. 'You *must* tell me!'

'I don't know what Rory's up to, Amy, and that's the truth,' he responded, falling silent as they passed by Ged Beresford's.

A finished coffin lay on the carpenter's sawhorses in readiness for the burial of Mary Pearson and her babe, who'd been lost in childbirth. 'Fanny's intended and his brother were in the Mermaid last night,' continued Dan at length. 'Being market day, the place was packed to the rafters, and they were playing cards with Collie Barraclough and a few other regulars. It was late, and I was surprised when I saw Rory walk in — he never comes into the Mermaid. He does his drinking out at the Green Man, and last night he'd already had a fair few, from the looks of him. Anyhow, next thing, the younger brother was standing out of the game and Rory was at the table playing. For high stakes, too.'

'Rory was gambling?' Amy's face fell. Pa would be furious if he found out! 'How could he afford to . . . Oh no! He got paid yesterday, Dan!'

'Aye, I guessed as much. It was all over pretty quick. Rory was outclassed — Theo Buxton's a sharp player. Better than he chooses to show, I fancy,' commented Dan matter-of-factly. 'Last I saw of Rory, he was sat in t'parlour with Buxton, talking real close over a smoke and a couple of whiskeys. I went for another barrel, and when I came back up both the brothers were at the card table again and Rory was gone.'

'He'd lost all his wages, yet he didn't come home,' pondered Amy, trying to make sense of it. 'Where is he? And why would he go to the Mermaid in the first place? Rory's scarcely been civil to Theo on the few occasions they've met, so what could they have been talking about?'

'The wedding, happen?' suggested Dan wryly. Moving ahead of her, he held the light high and shone it over the butcher's wall, scanning the blackness of the slaughter yard within. The Green Man stood a distance further ahead, and they walked all around the dilapidated tavern with its broken roofs and boarded-up windows without luck.

Finally turning towards the town once more, Dan suddenly veered away from Abbotsgate. 'He was already drunk. Had lost his wages playing cards,' he muttered, taking off through one of the winding ginnels. 'There's a place Rory might've gone to lick his wounds and drown his sorrows . . . '

'Where are we going?' exclaimed Amy, having to run to keep up with him as he strode through the maze of squalid alleys crammed with mean dwellings. She almost fell over a woman curled up and snoring against some railings. 'I've never been here before.'

'I should hope not!' Dan returned drily, all the time shining the light and searching. 'Look into the doorways and corners, Amy. That's where the girls take . . . Well, just look.'

They'd scarcely gone twenty yards further into the depths of Tanners Row, with Dan glancing down each set of stone steps to the cellars of the sordid buildings, when he spotted something and raised the lantern for a better look. 'Amy! Over here!'

Immediately at his side, Amy pressed

her hand to her mouth to stifle her cry. In the lanterns' guttering light, she could make out a crumpled figure sprawled upon the cobbles close to the midden wall. Before Dan could hold her back, Amy was on her knees at Rory's side. Fearfully, she touched a hand to his cold skin, gently smoothing the blood-matted lock of hair from his face, this time unable to prevent a cry of anguish escaping her lips.

'He's not dead, lass,' said Dan briskly, drawing Amy to her feet. 'Dead drunk is what he is.'

'But look at his face, Dan! And his hands!' She stooped and took one of Rory's rough, grimy hands in her own. 'He's cut and bleeding. He's been attacked, hasn't he?'

'Fighting, I'd say. And gave as good, likely better, than he got. I'd not care to see the other bloke,' remarked Dan, noting the grazes and bruising on Rory's fists and knuckles. Macfarlene was fast getting a name around Monks Quay for troublemaking and being too quick with his fists, but there was no cause for Amy to know that. Not before she had to, at any rate.

'We'll get him back to the Mermaid and sober him up,' grunted Dan, bending to the inert figure. 'He'll get to the clay pits on time whether he likes it or not!'

It was a long walk down Abbotsgate back to the inn. Rory didn't stir as Dan half-carried and half-dragged him along, finally propping him against the horse trough in the Mermaid's yard.

'Are you sure he'll be all right?' fretted Amy, her fingertips gently touching Rory's swollen cheekbone and bloody jaw. 'I'll bathe his face.'

'You'll do no such thing. You're worn out and chilled to the bone — go in to the fire and get yourself some hot tea. I'll see to Sleeping Beauty,' said Dan, filling a bucket from the pump. 'He'll be in a foul mood when he comes to, so don't expect any thanks.'

Amy did as she was bidden, grateful for the warmth and respite. She'd never actually been inside the Mermaid Inn before, even though it was a perfectly respectable establishment with a fine reputation for good food and hospitality. The inn had been in Dan Ainsworth's family for generations, and as well as local folk, was host to merchants, traders and ladies and gentlemen arriving in coaches from all over the county and much further afield.

Presently, Dan called Amy out to the stable yard, where she found Rory dripping wet and scowling, leaning back against the mounting block.

'Are you all right?' she asked him.

'What the blazes are you doing here?' He glowered up at her, spitting as he staggered to his feet, then reeling and stumbling back to the ground. 'Don't just stand there, girl! Help me up!'

However, even as Amy moved towards him, Rory lashed out and shoved her aside. Rolling clumsily to his left, he struggled to remove his boot and tipped out a heavy purse. Using his teeth to wrench open the drawstrings, he emptied the contents into the palm of his cupped hand.

Amy gasped. She'd never seen so much money!

'Nowt to do with you, Amy!' he hissed, replacing his boot and scrambling to his feet. 'Keep quiet about it or you'll be sorry!'

Dan Ainsworth stepped between brother and sister. 'Watch that temper, Rory!'

'Out of my way,' he squared up to Dan. 'What I said to her goes double for you!'

'Ah, don't make an even bigger fool of yourself,' said Dan in disgust. He turned away, and in that instant Rory lunged at him.

A scream choked Amy's throat as the two men crashed to the ground, rolling over and over in the cobbled yard. Although neither as tall nor muscular, on that morning Dan was the stronger and managed to overpower Rory, hauling him to his feet and pushing him back hard against the inn's wall.

'Get yourself along to the clay pits,'

he muttered, breathing hard. 'And be glad you've still a job to go to!'

'Go to hell!' Rory spat blood, striding across the stable yard without a backward glance. 'Go to hell, the pair of you!' He passed through the archway onto Abbotsgate and was gone from their sight.

Suddenly, Amy was trembling violently. Rory had always been hot-headed, but this . . .

'He'll have calmed down by the time he gets to the pits,' Dan reassured her, moving to her side. 'I wouldn't pay any heed to his threats. It's last night's ale talking. I'll fetch the wagon and drive you home.'

The sun was rising as Dan harnessed the stocky brown horse, and the wagon trundled out through the archway into Abbotsgate. The market town was soon left far behind and they rattled on westwards between the fields, finally reaching the rough shore track leading to Clockmakers Cottage. Unbidden, Rory's bruised and bloodied face swam once more into Amy's mind, and she glanced back to the distant spirals of smoke rising from the chimneys of Monks Quay. What on earth had Rory done in town last night? However had he come by so much money? She was cold with fear for whatever trouble he'd got himself into. And trouble it must surely be, for Rory to have possession of so many sovereigns!

2

Amy was sitting in the bay window alcove at the far end of the south-facing landing, making the most of the clear afternoon light. Her days at Whiteladies Grange were settled into a not unpleasant routine, and these hours after luncheon and before tea, when the housework was done and she was dressed in her black dress and frilled white cap and apron so as to be presentable above stairs, were her favourite time. She'd taken her sewing basket and bundle of mending into the window seat, and as soon as the buttons, hems and a cigar burn in the table linen were discreetly and invisibly repaired, she took out her coloured silks, picking up the dresser runner she was embroidering for the youngest Paslew daughter.

So engrossed was she in her work that she was unaware of Eleanor Paslew approaching along the landing, and started, jabbing herself with the fine needle when the tall, angular woman spoke to her.

'Oh, I beg your pardon, ma'am!' Amy was at once on her feet and bobbing a polite curtsey. 'I didn't hear — '

'That's quite all right, Amy. Do carry on with your sewing.' Mrs Paslew smiled and sat down beside her on the window seat. 'How are you settling in at Whiteladies?'

'Everybody's been very kind to me, ma'am,' the girl replied diffidently. 'I-I like working here very much.'

'I'm pleased to hear it. Mrs Braithwaite tells me you perform your duties diligently, are always willing, and have a good memory for your chores.'

'I write down a list of things Mrs Braithwaite tells me to do,' said Amy, and at once she bit her tongue, wondering if she'd spoken out of turn. Hadn't Fanny warned her that many mistresses didn't like their servants being able to read and write? 'It helps me to remember, ma'am. Is that all right?'

'Indeed it is.' The warmth of Mrs Paslew's smile reached her eyes, transforming her plain face. 'I write as an *aide de memoir* myself, and would expect nothing less than perfect literacy from a niece and former pupil of Anne Shawcross. So how is your aunt, Amy? Apart from church, I'm afraid I hardly ever see Anne now. Our paths have seldom crossed these past years, yet we were great friends when we were young. Did you know that?'

Amy's soft brown eyes glanced fleetingly up from her needlework. 'No, ma'am.'

'We were in the choir together at All Hallows, too. My father was vicar at that time. I knew your dear mother, too, of course,' added Mrs Paslew gently. 'Although not so very well, because Caroline was considerably younger than Anne and me.'

Amy nodded, unsure what to say. Apart from her interview for the position at Whiteladies, she hadn't had occasion to speak to Eleanor Paslew at all. Suddenly she realised the mistress was keenly watching her as she sewed.

'May I see?' Mrs Paslew extended a slender hand and spread the creamy embroidered linen across her lap, examining the neat needlework depicting an ornate little gate set into the corner of a walled garden filled with flowers. 'When I told you to make a runner for Clementine's dresser and that you might choose the design, I had in mind a simple pattern of decorative edging. It never occurred to me you would attempt anything as elaborate as this.'

Amy felt flustered, worried she'd overstepped her place. 'I'm sorry, ma'am. It's just, well, while I was thinking about which stitches and patterns to use, I saw Miss Clementine sitting reading in the walled garden beside the gate and so . . . ' Her voice trailed off. She just couldn't afford to lose her job at Whiteladies! 'I'm really sorry, ma'am. I haven't opened any new silks from the box. I've only used up ones already open, and — '

'That's of no concern, child; you must use whatever materials you require,' Mrs Paslew interrupted mildly. 'That particular corner of the walled garden has been Clementine's favourite place since she was a very small child. To portray it on her runner was thoughtful, and I'm certain Clementine will be delighted. It's beautiful work, Amy.'

'Thank you, ma'am. Ma was a fine needlewoman, and she taught Fanny and me, but Fanny is much better.'

'You've drawn the design cleverly,' went on Mrs Paslew, studying the girl's animated face. 'Can you tell me the names of the stitches you're using?'

'They're all quite simple ones, really,' responded Amy, her shyness melting as she smoothed out the linen cloth before them. 'Stem stitches for the flower stalks and some of the leaves. Satin for the fuller, bigger leaves here and here. Daisy, long and short, and straight stitches for all the flowers. French knots for the buds and thicker satin stitches in the gate, garden wall and for the little bird on the branch — although I haven't started her yet.'

'You don't use a hoop, even though there is one in the box?'

'I can work this pattern better without one, ma'am.'

'I see. If you require anything that isn't in the sewing box, you must say so, and it shall be ordered for you from the haberdasher in Liverpool. Do you understand?'

'Yes, ma'am.'

'I have an idea that when my other daughters see Clementine's new runner, you'll be kept busy sewing for them too. Will you mind that, Amy?'

'Oh, no! I love sewing. Especially fancy, pretty things like this.'

'I must have a word with Mrs Braithwaite, so you may be allowed a little more time for needlework. The drawing-room would benefit from new cushions, I fancy.' She rose from the window seat. 'Is your father ashore at present?'

'No, ma'am. Pa's been away these past weeks. He's due home with the tide early this evening.'

'Ah, yes. I recall Mr Paslew mentioning the packet was returning today. I daresay there's much for you to do at home in readiness for tomorrow's celebrations?'

'Aunt Anne's helping us with the dressmaking and the cooking. She's done ever so much baking.'

'That sounds like Anne! I'm sure it will be a wonderful wedding. Your sister and Theodore make a charming couple. It's been a delight having him and Nicholas staying with us, and Gilbert home from university at last. I do like it when this old house is lively and filled with young people.' Eleanor Paslew turned and started along the wide landing. 'Be sure to go into the kitchen and see Mrs Braithwaite before you leave this evening, won't you, Amy.'

'Yes, ma'am,' she replied, hoping against hope that Gladys Braithwaite wouldn't have a long list of chores for her to complete before letting her go for the night.

As soon as the light began fading, she tidied away the sewing basket and dutifully went downstairs into the kitchen. 'Will there be anything else, Mrs Braithwaite?'

'Nowt that won't wait 'til you come up first thing in morning, lass,' replied Gladys Braithwaite, looking up from her pastry-making to a thin-faced girl sanding pans at the sink. 'Maisie, fetch that hamper from the pantry — and don't trail sand all across my clean floor while you're doing it! The missus asked me to put up a few treats for the marriage feast,' she went on to Amy, as the scullery maid returned with a large basket. 'There's pies, potted meats and suchlike, a big tipsy cake and some fruit jellies. I put in a couple of my special mulled puddings for good measure. One's for eating after the wedding, and t'other to keep for the birth of their first child.'

'How thoughtful!' exclaimed Amy, raising the linen cloth and peeking into the laden basket. 'Fanny will be delighted — she's so keen for tomorrow to be really special for everyone.'

'It'll be special in more ways than one,' remarked Mrs Braithwaite sagely. 'Likely the last time the Macfarlenes'll be together. Nowt will be the same once Fanny's wed and gone.'

'She'll only be in York, Mrs Braithwaite!' protested Amy, more cheerfully than she felt. 'Theodore's family home is near the minster, in Carteret Square.'

'Never heard of it nor been there,' returned the older woman, her plump fingers deftly decorating the pastry crusts with scallops and twists. 'You can't walk it, and that makes it far enough away enough for you to lose touch quick as snap. A shame Mr Buxton won't have any family of his own at his wedding, isn't it?' she went on casually, glancing sidelong at Amy. 'Apart from his brother standing for him, of course. Unusual, too. Folk of quality generally have hordes of kith and kin turning up at their weddings, don't they?'

'Mr Buxton — Theodore — lost his father last year. The family are still in mourning. Lavish celebrations wouldn't have been appropriate, Mrs Braithwaite,' replied Amy stiffly. As well as cooking and managing the household at Whiteladies Grange, Gladys Braithwaite kept busy gossiping and prying into other folks' affairs. Crossing her fingers firmly behind her back, Amy added, 'Besides, Fanny wanted a quiet wedding.'

'Would've thought a big society do'd be more to your Fanny's taste,' sniffed the cook. 'She always has such a fine air about her.'

'Everyone says she's done right well for herself catching the likes of Mr Buxton,' chipped in Maisie unexpectedly, looking up from her pans. 'Him being a gentleman and all, and her just a common seafarer's daughter.'

'I think Fanny and Theo are both very lucky to have found each other and be marrying tomorrow,' responded Amy with a smile to the little scullery maid Maisie was but eleven or twelve years old, and Amy realised the girl was only repeating comments she'd heard from her elders, Gladys Braithwaite doubtless among them. Picking up the hamper, Amy started from the kitchen. 'Goodnight. See you in the morning.'

Swiftly changing from her black cotton dress into her own clothes and wrapping a shawl about her shoulders, Amy lost no time scurrying out across the drying green away from the house and around the tall yew hedge — only to collide with Nicholas Buxton, who was standing in the middle of the path staring off inland towards the hills.

'Oh!' she exclaimed.

'I do beg your pardon!' he apologised at once, reaching out to steady her. 'I'm most awfully sorry, Amy.'

'My fault, Mr Nicholas,' she replied, balancing the hamper, straightening her hat and managing to bob a curtsey all at once. 'I wasn't looking where I was going.'

'Nonsense! You weren't expecting to turn the hedge and find some melancholy ass blocking your path,' he returned firmly. 'And Amy, can't you please call me Nicholas — or Nick, even? After all, this time tomorrow we'll be family.'

She smiled up at him. From the little she knew of the Buxton brothers, they could hardly have been more different in temperament as well as appearance. Theodore was tall and muscular with features almost as dark as a gypsy's, whereas Nicholas was slightly built, pale of countenance and reddish-haired. The starkest contrast was between the brothers' characters, however, the younger being mild-mannered — shy, almost, and the elder urbane, dominant and somehow unprincipled. Their acrimonious argument from the previous evening flashed vividly into Amy's thoughts, her disquiet clearly revealed upon her expressive face.

'Are you all right?' Nicholas queried at once, wresting the heavy hamper from her arms. 'Let me take this. Are you on your way home?'

'Yes, but I can manage, really,' she protested. 'It's not far. I take the short-cut through Friars Wood and across — '

'Then I'll walk with you,' he interrupted gently. 'Truth to tell, Amy, I'll be glad for your company. I'm weary of being alone with my thoughts.'

A rather awkward silence lengthened between them as they crossed the park from Whiteladies Grange, winding down towards the wood with its old trees and fresh green foliage. Amy was racking her brains for something to say, when Nicholas gestured expansively towards the cloudless sky and surrounding landscape.

'Thank goodness the weather's been pleasant today!' he exclaimed. 'There's little worse than a cold wet picnic, and the weather looked far from promising when Theo set off to collect Fanny.'

'I didn't know they were going out today.'

'Spur-of-the-moment arrangement, I

think,' went on Nicholas. 'We were out riding this morning, and Theo asked Gilbert where there was a pleasing place for a picnic. He immediately recommended somewhere called St Agnes Falls. Said it was beautiful. 'Incredibly beautiful and tranquil' were his exact words. Do you know it?'

'Mmm. Ma used to take us there sometimes when we were small. It *is* lovely, especially at this time of year,' she replied, rather surprised someone like Gilbert Paslew would even be aware of such an out-of-the-way spot. 'There's a dell beneath the falls that's filled with flowers the whole summer long.'

'According to Gilbert, there are some quite rare plants and grasses growing there, too,' went on Nicholas amiably. 'He was telling us something about a holy spring from ancient times. Long ago, monks were travelling through Lancashire and they stopped for the night in the woods. At dawn they saw a vision at the spring, and that was why

they decided to establish their monas-
tery here in Monks Quay. Then later
the sisters came, and Whiteladies
Grange was built. Although it wasn't
called Whiteladies Grange in those
days, of course.'

'I didn't know any of that,' said Amy.
'I've never heard that story. How
wonderful!'

'Oh, Gilbert knows all sorts of things.
He's a frightfully clever chap. Always
was. He'd help me with my prep at
school, and Gil had this odd way of
making even really boring things like
theology and philosophy seem quite
lively. I muddled through, thanks to
him.' Nicholas grinned at her as they
clambered over the stile into Friars
Wood. 'I'm pretty much a duffer
— Theo has the brains in our family!'

'I enjoyed school — my Aunt Anne
has been a teacher here all her life
— and I do like learning things, but my
brother Edmund's the clever one. He's
always studying and hopes to get a
scholarship. Did you meet Mr Gilbert

at school, or have your families always known each other?'

'Gracious, no!' Nicholas said with a laugh. 'Father was posted to India as a very young man, and that's where he met and married my mother. She was from an army family, too. Neither one of them has — had — set foot on English soil for more than thirty years. I doubt very much if Mother will ever make the journey now. She's not strong, and since Father died . . . ' He smiled sadly. 'India and the regiment have been my mother's whole life. Her friends and home are there.'

'It must've been very hard to leave your parents and come to school in a strange country,' Amy remarked sympathetically. 'I can't bear even the thought of leaving my family and home.'

'It's not the done thing to own up to, but I was pretty miserable as a boy,' conceded Nicholas. 'I mean, Theo's the best brother anybody could wish for, and he did his best to look out for me. It's always been Theo and me against the world! But because he was eight years my senior, we weren't able to see much of each other during term time. Holidays were all right. We spent those together at the school, with other boys whose folk were abroad.'

'You didn't go home to India at all? It must've been such a lonely life!'

'Oh, it wasn't so bad. Just the way things are, I suppose,' he returned brightly. 'Although everything bucked up no end once I got to know Gilbert. He's a fine friend. The Paslews started inviting me to spend holidays with them at Whiteladies. Theo had long since left school and was back in India with the diplomatic corps by then. Even after we grew up and Gil went to Oxford, he and I have remained the best of pals.'

'Last summer, when Theo met Fanny,' ventured Amy, 'was that the first time he'd been to Whiteladies?'

'Yes, it was.' Nicholas gazed straight ahead, beyond the meadows and down to the shimmering ribbon of sea. 'We had a wonderful visit, and as you know, were invited back for Christmas and the New Year. Theo and Mr Paslew get on like a house on fire.' A frown creased his forehead. 'Things in common, I suppose. Business and suchlike. They talk together for hours on end.' He met her eyes urgently as they passed through the back gate of Clockmakers Cottage and started up through the garden towards the kitchen door. 'Amy, have you ever done something and later wished you hadn't? And — and then not done something you knew full well you should have to put it right? Then suddenly it's far too late and you've done nothing, not a thing, to stop the wrong and set things right?' He looked distractedly away from her, his voice dropping. 'No, of course you haven't. Only I could be such a fool.'

Vicky burst from the cottage and hurtled towards them. 'You're back! What's in the big basket, Amy? Is it for Fanny's wedding? Can I see?'

'Not until Fanny gets home,' replied Amy. She bent to hug her young sister, but her gaze never left Nicholas Buxton as he stepped into the cool larder and set down the wedding hamper. 'Nicholas — '

'I'd best be off.' He forced a smile, tipping his hat and moving out into the garden once more. 'I shouldn't have . . . Just ignore me! Theo often tells me I fuss and fume too much over things, and I'm sure he's right.'

'Please,' she persisted quietly, walking with him to the gate, 'won't you at least come in for a cup of tea?'

He shook his head and smiled down at her. 'Best be getting back. Thank you for our walk, Amy. I enjoyed it. And our conversation.'

'I did, too.' Even as the words left her lips, Nicholas Buxton was walking up through the meadows towards Friars Wood, leaving Amy filled with questions and Vicky tugging at her skirts and pulling at her hands.

'Aunt Anne's ironing my dress for tomorrow, and we've made cherry biscuits — I cut them out myself!' The little girl broke free, running on ahead. 'Come and see! Hurry!'

Amy dutifully followed, pausing at the apple tree where Edmund was sitting and reading. 'Any sign of Rory?' she asked him.

He shook his head, looking up from his book. 'What was all that about with Nicholas Buxton?'

She sighed, starting indoors. 'I only wish I knew!'

★   ★   ★

The Monks Quay packet was due home with the evening tide, and Vicky was up in the sisters' room watching from under the eaves for the first glimpse of Pa's boat on the horizon. Amy and Aunt Anne were in the cottage's comfortable sitting-room, winding wool and relishing the peace.

'We should get that clock packed up tonight,' commented Anne Shawcross, nodding to the fine walnut corner clock made by her great-grandfather as a wedding gift for his bride. Shawcrosses had made clocks in this very room since the 1690s, the craft being passed from father to son down the years until Anne's generation, when only daughters were born to the family. A century and more of skill and tradition duly died and were buried with their father. 'There won't be time to fuss with it tomorrow.'

'I wish Ma were here to pass the clock on to Fanny,' mused Amy. 'That clock always reminds me of Ma. She loved it so.'

'I do myself,' admitted Anne. 'Caroline and I grew up with its tick and chime, and Father making a ceremony of winding it up each night on his way to bed. After your grandparents died and your mother and I were living here alone, I'd sometimes just sit here in this room listening to the clock, imagining all the years and the lives and the faces it has seen passing. I was still quite young then, with a fair share of fanciful notions.'

'I hadn't ever realised, or even thought about it before,' remarked Amy softly. 'But you really do love this cottage, don't you, Aunt Anne? Every bit as much as I do.'

'I was born and grew up here. All my happy memories are within these walls,' she answered simply. 'Although I haven't lived here for more than twenty years, I suppose I still think of Clockmakers Cottage as home.'

'It must've broken your heart to leave it and move into the schoolhouse.'

'Don't be melodramatic, child.' She shook her head, tying off a bobbin. 'Caroline had a husband and a baby on the way. It was only right and proper that her family should have the cottage to themselves, especially since the schoolhouse was standing empty with the school on its doorstep. No more treks back and forth into town. It was far more convenient all round.' She broke off and looked up. 'Vicky's very quiet, isn't she? I'd better see what she's up to.'

'I'll go.' Amy rose, just as there was a shriek from above. Vicky clattered down the steep stairs.

'Is it Pa's boat?' Amy asked her.

'No, only Fanny and Theodore coming in the carriage.' Vicky screwed up her face, thinking. 'Amy, I've waited and *waited* for Pa to come, and he hasn't. I don't think he can find his way home this time!'

'Of course he can, pet,' said Amy with a smile. 'Why wouldn't he?'

'Because it's daylight!' persisted Vicky. 'There aren't any stars, are there? If the Dog Star's not shining, Pa won't know which way to sail, will he?'

Aunt Anne cast an I-told-you-so glance at Amy, who was lost for words. Amy's fairy story about the big bright Dog Star lighting up the sky so Pa could see his way home at night had soothed Vicky's bedtime fears about her father getting lost at sea in the dark. The comforting tale had done the trick. And it had seemed such a good idea at the time.

'Erm, Pa can see his way home today, pet. He doesn't need the Dog Star when it's still light like this. Now, you know how much Pa likes asparagus — shall we gather some for his homecoming supper?'

'Dog Star indeed!' tutted Aunt Anne, peering over her spectacles at Amy when Vicky had thumped out for her boots. 'That child is going to grow up with a distorted view of the natural world — you just mark my words.'

★ ★ ★

Ramsay Macfarlene was ashore safe and sound and the table set for supper when Rory came in, and from the look of him Amy was reassured he had indeed spent that day working up at Paslew's clay pits.

He dismissed his father's questions about his bruised and swollen face, setting down to his meal. 'Had a scrap with a bloke up at t'pits. Summat and nowt.'

'You're not a lad anymore, Rory. It's high time you grew up and started using your brain instead of your fists,' was all Ramsay said, but Amy knew full well it was only because Pa didn't want to spoil the happy occasion of the family's homecoming supper that he wasn't tearing a strip off her brother and demanding explanations.

Straight after the meal, Rory snatched up his coat and strode out again. It wasn't until the dishes were cleared and washed, Vicky tucked up and asleep, Edmund studying, Fanny mixing honey and fine oatmeal into a concoction for her face, and Aunt Anne returned to the schoolhouse, that Ramsay went out into the garden and gathered an armful of summer flowers.

'Amy, I'm off to see your ma.'

'Mind if I come?' She smiled across at him, already untying her apron. 'I'll just fetch my bonnet.'

The quarter-moon was rising above them as they turned their backs upon the sea and started towards All

Hallows, its square bell tower and surmounting cross silhouetted against the velvety night sky. It was the first chance they'd had to talk properly.

'Was everything all right, Pa? With the *Jenet Rae*?'

'She needs repair, Amy. A boat's like a living thing. It needs proper looking after, and Alfred Paslew just don't care. That's the truth of it.'

'Is it dangerous?' she persisted anxiously. 'Whatever it is that needs fixing?'

Ramsay weighed his words. 'The *Jenet Rae* isn't as seaworthy as she could be, lass. If we hit certain weather or seas, she could get into difficulties. I told Paslew as much after the last voyage, and the one before that, but all he cares about is a fast buck. He's not a seaman and he's got no interest in the *Jenet Rae*. Never had, and never will.'

Amy shook her head, perplexed. 'Why did he bother buying her at all?'

'Because the *Jenet Rae* is another piece of Monks Quay for him to own,' returned Ramsay tersely. 'After old

Spencer died, his widow didn't want the boat or the business. The poor woman just wanted shot of the whole caboodle and enough money to move away to live with her daughter in Douglas. Paslew saw the chance of a bargain and he snapped it up. Happen he won't be satisfied till he owns the whole town, and everyone in it!'

They reached the lichgate of All Hallows, and Ramsay removed his hat as they walked down the winding path towards the church. 'I'm truly glad Fanny's getting married, and I hope she'll be very happy,' murmured Amy, slipping her arm through her father's. 'I just wish she was staying here with us in Monks Quay instead of going so far away.'

'A wife's place is with her husband, Amy. Theo's not our class. He belongs to a different world. There's nothing here for him. I did have my doubts about him and Fanny at first, but they look a good match. And Fanny never would've been happy wed to a local lad and living in Monks Quay, y'know.'

'I suppose not.' She smiled as they neared the west door. Ma rested across the churchyard in the far corner beneath the willows. Pa always visited her as soon as he got home from the sea. 'I'll go inside to wait for you.'

'Thanks, lass.' He kissed her forehead. 'I'll not be long.'

She watched his figure receding into the soft summer darkness before she stepped inside the porch. Her hand was upon the round handle of the west door when the sound of voices from within caused her to hesitate. If Reverend Linley was in church speaking with a parishioner, she didn't wish to intrude. Booted footsteps approached the door, scraping on the stone-flagged nave, and as the voices of two men drew nearer and more distinct, Amy recognised both. Rory and Theodore Buxton!

The handle turned from inside and Amy shrank back into the deep shadows, her heart hammering. The heavy door was pulled open and the men emerged, striding across the porch. Clearly they had concluded their conversation within the sacred confines of the church, for not another word passed between them. Descending the steps, they each went their separate ways; Theodore Buxton towards the east gate, where a bridle path led through the woods to Whiteladies Grange, and Rory vanishing swiftly into the night in the direction of the Green Man tavern.

⋆   ⋆   ⋆

It was a beautiful wedding. Everyone said so. After the register was signed, and the bells were rung and the rice and rose petals thrown, the newlyweds drove in the Paslews' carriage down to Clockmakers Cottage with their guests following on foot, horseback and cart.

The summer afternoon was fine and warm, so the wedding feast was set out in the garden, where the happy couple were toasted and well-wished with ale and cider presented by the Ainsworth family, and fruit cordial from Aunt Anne's kitchen.

Amy wasn't sure if Pa had given Rory a good talking-to, but her brother had been on his best behaviour all day. He'd been polite and amiable to everybody and had even borrowed a penny whistle to join the fiddlers, flute and squeeze-box playing reels and jigs for the dancing. Folk who weren't dancing were drifting about the garden, drinking and chatting.

It had been a lovely day, reflected Amy from her quiet seat beneath the apple tree. Fanny had never looked more radiant, nor Pa so proud. Ma would've —

'A penny for them.'

She started, squinting up through the dappled sunlight to find Dan Ainsworth beaming down at her. 'I bet your thoughts were worth more than that,' he laughed.

'I was remembering past times.' She smiled, gazing wistfully around at her mother's garden. 'It's funny how things from long, long ago seem so bright and near.'

'I know exactly what you mean.' Steadying his tankard of ale, Dan dropped to his knees, stretching out on the grass at Amy's feet. 'I remember Uncle Bruce sailing in from America like it was yesterday. I was only a little lad, yet I can recall all his tales about New York and Chicago and being a newspaperman.' He narrowed his eyes, looking up at her against the sun. 'I don't suppose you remember Uncle Bruce, do you?'

Amy shook her head. It was peculiar — since they'd left school, she and Dan had merely exchanged pleasantries whenever they met in the town, yet now it was somehow as if they were the closest of friends. 'Do you still want to be a newspaperman like your uncle?'

'Why, Amy, I'm amazed you remember! It's years ago I told you that. When we were sat together on the back row of your Aunt Anne's schoolroom, wasn't it?'

She lowered her eyes, glancing away to where Pa was taking his turn at throwing horseshoes. 'It was on our last day at school, and Aunt Anne asked us to write an essay about what we'd most like to do in our lives.' Amy met his gaze with a smile. 'You were always really good at writing.'

'Much good it's done me so far!' He sighed. 'But aye, I'd still like to do it. Da's all for me taking over the Mermaid one day, just as he did from his da. That's the trouble with small towns like Monks Quay, y'know. You're brought up to do exactly what your da done, whether you like it or not.'

'And you don't like it?'

He swirled the ale around his tankard, considering. 'It's not that, exactly. It's just I'd like to do something different. I reckon I *could* write for a newspaper, given half the chance. And it's not like I'm the only son, is it? Amos or Sam could just as easy run the Mermaid. When they're old enough, of course.'

'Would you sail to America, as your uncle did?'

'Maybe. I'd like to go to all the places he writes to me about.' Dan paused, watching a ladybird settle momentarily upon the toe of Amy's satin slipper before fluttering away. 'I see the ocean every day of my life, Amy. I look out across all that water and think there's a whole world out there. I want to see some of it before I die.'

'You sound exactly like Fanny! She always wanted to get away,' said Amy with a laugh. 'I look across the sea, too, but I've never ever wanted to sail away. This is my home; everything that's important to me is here. I want to stay in Monks Quay always.'

'I could be happy here. Lancashire has good newspapers, so I wouldn't need to go away to be a newspaperman.' Dan met and held her gaze as he raised the tankard to his lips. 'Nor would I, if I had reason enough to stay.'

'Isn't — ' began Amy, breaking off as Fanny rustled towards them, still wearing her wedding dress.

'Do forgive me for interrupting you,

Dan, but Theo and I are soon to leave.' She beamed down at them, her eyes sparkling mischievously. 'I need to steal Amy from you for just a little while. I'm sure she'll return directly.'

'What was all that about?' hissed Amy, when the sisters were indoors and going up to their room. 'You made it sound like — '

'Exactly!' Fanny swept into the room and whisked off her bonnet, sitting before the glass so Amy could fix her hair. 'Dan Ainsworth is smitten with you, Amy — that much is obvious. There's no need to be coy,' she went on, surveying her sister's flushed face through the mirror. 'The boy was sweet on you even at school — I clearly recall telling you so.'

'Fanny, for goodness sake!' Amy busied herself with the combs and pins. 'I suppose Dan *did* like me a bit then, but we were . . . we were only children!'

'Well, he certainly isn't a child any longer.' Fanny arched an eyebrow, smoothing a ringlet around her finger.

'Nor are you. You could do a lot worse than Dan Ainsworth, Amy. He's just about the only man in Monks Quay with an ounce of spark. Don't risk losing him.' Fanny turned to face her younger sister earnestly. 'If you do, you'll regret it for the rest of your life!'

* * *

'My wife and I are driving up to Whiteladies Grange to pay our respects to the Paslews,' Theodore was explaining to Mrs Ainsworth and the gaggle of ladies clustered around him in the garden. 'My brother is staying on at Whiteladies for another month, while Fanny and I are travelling directly to Pemberley for our honeymoon. Mr Paslew is very generously allowing us the use of his coach and man for the journey. Ah, here is my bride!' He beamed as Fanny emerged from the cottage in a becoming rose madder skirt and jacket. 'Am I not the most fortunate man alive, ladies?'

Fanny paused on the threshold, turning

to give Amy a quick hug. 'If you hadn't stepped in to look after the family, I could never have married Theo,' she whispered, blinking back sudden tears. 'Thank you so much, dear Amy!'

'It's what I wanted to do,' mumbled Amy. 'Oh, Fan, I will miss you!'

'And I you. But York really isn't so far away. You must visit soon.' Both sisters smiled confidently and nodded, each knowing this would be their last meeting for a very long time. Perhaps forever.

'You mustn't worry, Amy. About the responsibility of the home and family, I mean,' continued Fanny softly. 'You'll manage splendidly. You're far more like Ma and her ways than I ever was. Everything will be fine, you'll see!'

Then suddenly she was gone, out into the sunlit garden, with cheers and good-byes ringing out around Clockmakers Cottage as Theodore Buxton handed his new wife up into the Paslews' elegant open carriage with its tasteful festoons of satin ribbons, creamy white hothouse blooms and glossy dark green foliage.

Holding her bridal posy in both hands, Fanny turned away from the well-wishers gathered about the carriage; and although she closed her eyes tightly, the flowers flew unerringly in Amy's direction. She caught them tentatively, and another cheer went up as she buried her warm face in their sweet fragrance. Theo jingled the reins, and another shower of rice and petals fluttered about the newlyweds as the gleaming bay shook her mane and moved sedately away upon the short journey to Whiteladies Grange.

'I'm glad you caught the bunch of flowers, lass,' said Pa. 'I thought that sister of yours was going to throw them at me! Now, where's Dan — ? Ah, Dan! We're setting up another round of horseshoes. Are you in?'

Dan Ainsworth gazed at Amy, who was standing a little way from everyone with the bridal flowers still in her arms. He drew a breath to make comment, then thought better of it and turned toward Ramsay. 'You, me, Amos and Ned Yarkin, is it? Aye, count me in!'

* ★ ★

Dusk was falling before the last of the merry-makers made their way home from Clockmakers Cottage. Vicky was already fast asleep in her bed, worn out after the excitement of the day. As she stood at the kitchen window washing the final few dishes, Amy absently watched Pa accompanying Ned Yarkin to the gate. The Mermaid's elderly pot-man had drunk and feasted well and was in fine fettle, doubtless setting the world to rights or expounding upon some subject Amy was too far away to hear. Suddenly though, she saw Pa wheel sharply to face Mr Yarkin, steadying the old man's shambling gait and addressing him intently. Ned Yarkin merely shook his head, clapped Ramsay on the shoulder a couple of times, bade his friend and neighbour goodnight and ambled on his way.

Seconds later, Ramsay Macfarlene thundered into the cottage, his weather-beaten features grim and his pale blue eyes blazing. 'Where is he? Where's Rory?' he demanded of Amy. 'Ned Yarkin's just told me what happened in Monks Quay the other night. Why didn't you tell me, lass? Were you hoping I'd not find out?'

'No!' she exclaimed in horror. 'No, Pa! It wasn't like — '

'You're in charge of this household now, Amy,' he went on angrily. 'I can't be here all the time, so I depend on you to take responsibility for what goes on while I'm away. I won't have Rory disgracing the family! Now where *is* he — ?'

'I'm here, Pa.' Rory stood in the doorway from the stairs, the smouldering rage in his eyes more than matching his father's. 'And I'm going out, so say your piece and I'll be on my way.'

'You'll not go anywhere till I get some answers, my lad!' Ramsay raised an accusing finger. 'You lied to me, Rory, and I can't abide a liar! A scrap with a bloke at the clay pits, was it? 'Summat and nowt', you said! Well? I'm waiting for the truth!'

Amy saw Rory's jaw tighten. His eyes narrowed, and the malicious glance he threw in her direction chilled her to the bone. 'What I do is my business.'

'No it isn't, not while you're part of this family and living under my roof!' Ramsay banged the flat of his hand onto the scrubbed table, surveying his son in disgust. 'What's up with you, Rory? Starting trouble at that thieves' den the Green Man. Getting yourself drunk senseless and brawling in the street over a common — ' He broke off, mindful of Amy's presence and amending his words. 'Brawling over a girl of the town. Making a show of yourself in the Mermaid, gambling with men who could buy and sell you ten times over and losing your wages. A whole week's wages on the turn of a card!' Ramsay shook his head in disbelief. 'It's time you woke up to your responsibilities to this family! You've a duty to pay your way. How do you think your sister is to manage this week with no money from you?'

'She'll have to get used to it, won't

she? Because I don't intend being around here much longer anyhow!' Striding past them both, Rory wrenched open the cottage door and slammed it behind him. The anger drained visibly from Ramsay's face, and Amy was shocked at how old and tired her pa suddenly appeared.

'He lied to me, Amy,' mumbled Ramsay without looking at her. 'The rest, I could've . . . But my son *lied* to me!'

'I know. I know, Pa,' she murmured, already reaching for her shawl. 'I'm going after him.'

Amy had to run to catch up with Rory, snatching at his arm to halt his pace once she did so. 'Rory, I didn't — '

'Had to go running to Pa with tales about your bad big brother, didn't you?' Shaking loose of her grasp, he rounded on her, gripping her narrow shoulders so fiercely she cried out. 'One word about them sovereigns, and you'll find out just how bad I can be!' Shoving her roughly aside, he swiftly put distance between them. Amy hesitated in the twilight, uncertain whether to return home or follow him, to try to explain. And perhaps keep an eye on him, too, for such was his temper there was no guessing what he might do.

When instead of taking the road into town, Rory cut across country towards Whiteladies Grange, Amy's decision was made. What purpose could he have for going to Whiteladies, other than another clandestine meeting with Theodore Buxton before he and Fanny left for Pemberley? Amy followed her brother warily, fearful lest he take a backward glance and discover her. After a mile or so, Rory threw himself down into the coarse grass next to the stone slab, where in olden days the dead brought up from the sea and their bearers would rest on their way to the burial ground.

Pressing into the shadows of the hedgerow, Amy waited. It was not long before a lone horseman cantered into sight along the track and Amy's suspicions were confirmed. Theodore Buxton didn't dismount, but merely leaned down as Rory sprang to his feet and moved to the horse's side.

A few words were exchanged. Theodore handed a thick oblong package to Rory before sitting back in the saddle and gathering up the reins. He nodded, speaking as if issuing instructions; and as Amy watched, Theodore Buxton reached into his coat, withdrew a small object and passed this also to Rory.

Amy's breath constricted in her chest, for in the pale glow of moonlight she clearly saw the gleaming barrel of a snub pistol resting in her wayward brother's hands.

3

'Try not to worry, Amy,' Anne Shawcross said while they stood at the school-house window watching Vicky sitting cross-legged out in the early-morning sunshine. With elbows planted on her knees, she was intently watching the pollen-laden honeybees circling back and forth from their hives to the swaths of lavender, wild roses, clover and stocks abundant in Anne's neat garden. 'Although starting school is a daunting occasion for most children, I'm certain Vicky will take it in her stride.'

Amy's warm brown eyes were concerned and unconvinced. 'She's such a little girl, Aunt Anne.'

'It's true Vicky's rather young to be joining school. However, she's very bright for her years. Thanks to Fanny, she can already read and make the beginnings of her letters. Vicky won't be struggling to catch up with the others.'

'I'd wanted to keep her at home until Pa sails, so she could spend these last few days at Clockmakers with him,' said Amy soberly. 'But Pa thought it better she start school straight away.'

'I'm in absolute agreement with your father, which doesn't occur very often,' replied Anne wryly. 'All Vicky has known until now is being at the cottage and having Fanny with her virtually every minute of every day. Now that Fanny's married and gone, it's as well Vicky settles into the new routine of things before Ramsay leaves too.'

'I wish I could give up working at Whiteladies and stay at home to care for Vicky and the family, as Fanny did.'

'Could you afford to?'

Amy shook her head despondently. Despite Pa working hard all his life, first Ma and then Fanny had had to scrimp and save to make ends meet. And these past weeks, Rory had not contributed anything towards his keep. 'You know I lost all my brass playing cards,' he'd said with a shrug when Amy had tackled him about it. 'How can I give you what I don't have?' His sharp blue eyes had bored into hers, defying her to challenge him about that purse of sovereigns. Anxious not to stir up further trouble during Pa's short stay ashore, she'd held her tongue.

Now Amy met her aunt's gaze ruefully. 'We couldn't manage without my wages from Whiteladies. And I do enjoy working there, especially the sewing. Mrs Paslew's been ever so nice.'

'Eleanor Paslew's a good woman; always was. Do your best for her, and you'll not go far wrong.' She paused, eyeing her favourite niece keenly. 'What's troubling you, child? I know your father and I don't always get along — never have and never shall — but we *are* family. I want to help, if I can. Is it Rory? Have he and your father fallen out?'

'Pa and Rory did have a set-to the night of the wedding,' answered Amy honestly. 'If they've argued since, I haven't been there.'

On the rare occasions she'd seen her father and brother together at Clockmakers Cottage, there was stony silence and an atmosphere so tense it could be cut with a knife. Rory was behaving as if nothing untoward had happened, and Amy couldn't help wondering if he was deliberately keeping out of Pa's way and merely biding his time until Ramsay sailed before carrying out whatever deed he and Theodore Buxton had agreed upon that night at the resting place.

The burden of keeping silent about witnessing the exchange of package and pistol weighed heavily and constantly upon Amy. She longed for somebody to talk to, to confide in. How she missed Fanny!

★ ★ ★

A keen easterly wind blowing down from the hills whipped ruddy colour into Amy's cheeks as she hung out the laundry at Whiteladies Grange. Propping the billowing lines high on the drying green, she stooped to pick up the baskets and hurried through the wash-house into the hot, steamy kitchen.

'You'd best keep an eye out the window, Amy,' commented Gladys Braithwaite sagely. 'I feel rain in my bones. Now get them jars washed and dried quick as you can — I can't trust Maisie to do it. If I've told that girl once the jars have to be spotlessly clean and bone-dry or the preserves go mouldy, I've told her a hundred times, but she still don't do the job right. Where is she, anyway?'

'Filling the scuttles, I think.'

The cook tutted in exasperation, tipping soft fruits and diced crab apples into one of the huge jamming pans. 'I sent her to fetch the coal half an hour since! She's as slow on the move as she is on t'uptake. When you've a spare minute, I'll need more sugar grinding.'

Rolling up her sleeves, Amy drew the water and set it to boil before fetching the heavy wooden sugar box. Taking the hammer and flat blade, she cracked a generous slab from the loaf and broke it into smaller pieces before dropping them a handful at a time into the grinder. The basin of sparkling sugar granules was barely filled before the water bubbled to the boil. Hefting the tray of glass jars from the pantry's high shelf, she got started sorting and washing.

The rain held off long enough for the day's laundry to be almost dry before Amy had to dart out and hastily take it down from the lines, bundling it into the baskets and racing back indoors.

'I know nowt about it, Gladys!' Dobson, the head gardener, was sitting himself down at the kitchen table. 'Mind, I've not been in t'town this side of a fortnight.'

'Market day last week. That's when it happened. Edith Barraclough told me all about it when she brought the butter and eggs this morning,' said Mrs Braithwaite, pouring her old friend a cup of tea. 'Left for dead, was what she said!'

'Who was he?'

'Nobody local. I think Edie said his name was Sydney Wallace or some such. Middle-aged, portly. Travelling salesman, she reckoned. Collie's cowman found him crawling up the lane towards the farmhouse. In a terrible state, he was! Blood — ' She broke off, suddenly noticing Amy standing transfixed in the doorway from the wash-house. 'Don't just stand there gawping, girl! Get started preparing the vegetables Mr Dobson's brought, and sort the potatoes for roasting. You know by now the size I like them.'

Mrs Braithwaite cast a long-suffering glance in the head gardener's direction, topping up his cup as she did so. 'Another slice of my date and walnut cake, Mr Dobson? Now, where was I? Oh, aye. This Mr Wallace had been set upon on the drovers' road toward Preston, just beyond the Green Man.'

'It's a rough house, is that.' Dobson chewed on his cake. 'Any one of them as drinks up at t'Green Man is just as likely to slit your throat as wish you the time of day. Gang of them, was there?'

83

'Nay, just the one. Mr Wallace was riding along and the villain came out of the dark at him. Dragged Mr Wallace to the ground, gave him a right thumping, stole his money and took his horse!'

'Horse thieving.' Dobson shook his head grimly. 'You can hang for that, tha knows!'

'That's another queer thing — the robber didn't keep the horse. Edie said the day after poor Mr Wallace turned up at the farmhouse, one of the lads the Barracloughs have hired on to lift their spuds spotted his horse wandering by the river.'

'So this Wallace feller got his horse back then — I suppose that's summat.'

'No, he didn't, Mr Dobson! He'd already left Monks Quay on the first coach out. Didn't want to make a fuss, he said. Just wanted to get home to his wife and family. He even had to pawn his ring to pay for coach fare,' reflected Mrs Braithwaite, crumbling a bit of fruitcake between her plump fingers. 'Collie Barraclough had seen Wallace at the Mermaid the night he got robbed. He'd had his dinner there and played a couple of hands of cards with Collie and the others. When word got round town about what happened to him, Edie said Dan Ainsworth went looking all over for Mr Wallace.'

'What for? Why would young Dan be chasing this Wallace feller? Hadn't left the Mermaid without paying his bill, had he?'

'I don't know, do I? I only know what Edie Barraclough told me her Collie told her,' replied Mrs Braithwaite impatiently. 'Besides, whatever Dan Ainsworth wanted with Mr Wallace, he was too late to get it. Wallace had already left on the first coach.'

'It's a rum do, is that,' commented Dobson, rubbing his stubbly chin. 'Fancy a thief not taking a good horse!'

'Whole thing's queer, if you ask me,' sniffed Gladys Braithwaite, stirring another spoonful of sugar into her tea. 'When Wallace was robbed, he was heading toward Preston. Yet the coach he took was going to Liverpool. It's as if he couldn't get away from Monks Quay quick enough!'

'Dun't sound queer to me,' commented Dobson. 'I wouldn't want to hang round a place when I'd had the living daylights beaten out of me and all my money took.'

Amy's hands were deftly cleaning and preparing the vegetables Mr Dobson had gathered from Whiteladies' kitchen garden for that evening's dinner. Inwardly, however, she was reliving every moment of that awful morning when she and Dan found Rory in Monks Quay, and hearing over and over again the conversation between Gladys Braithwaite and Mr Dobson about a stranger who'd been attacked and robbed on the old drovers' road to Preston.

Until now, she'd believed Rory had been brawling in the town that night. That had to be the reason for his cuts and bruises, hadn't it? A middle-aged, portly man on his way home to his family would not be capable of trading blows and inflicting such wounds upon a strong young man like Rory. But where had the purse of sovereigns come from, if not the pocket of the travelling salesman?

Amy felt sick to her stomach. Surely her brother wasn't capable of attacking an innocent man and beating him within an inch of his life? She couldn't — *wouldn't* — believe it. And yet, it all fitted. And what of Dan Ainsworth? Why had he wished to speak so urgently to Mr Wallace? Dan had seen that purse of sovereigns every bit as clearly as Amy herself. Had he, too, put two and two together?

★   ★   ★

Amy's suspicions wormed deeper and deeper into her brain as that endless day wore on. She was anxious to talk to Dan, but Mrs Braithwaite had been in a crotchety mood all day long and Amy was convinced she'd be kept late at Whiteladies Grange that night.

'Amy! Have you got cloth ears or what?' The cook glared across the hot kitchen at her. 'The next batch is right for bottling. It'll not jump into the jars by itself!'

With the huge jamming pan on the table between them, the two women were ladling scalding-hot strawberry preserve into warmed glass jars when the door from the passageway swung open and Miss Sophie strode into the kitchen.

'Excuse me, Mrs Braithwaite,' the Paslews' middle daughter said, beaming brightly. 'I need to borrow Amy.'

'She's not dressed for upstairs, miss,' Gladys Braithwaite replied.

'I don't care about that.' She turned her attention to Amy. 'Come along!'

'Beg pardon, Miss Sophie, but Amy has to stay here with me,' persisted Mrs Braithwaite. 'We're bottling, and it's not a job as can wait. It has to be done while the fruit is piping hot.'

'I'm sure anybody can do that with you, Mrs B,' returned Sophie dismissively. 'I need Amy for something important.' The tall young woman turned on her heel.

Unsure whether to follow or stay put, Amy glanced at Mrs Braithwaite. The cook pursed her lips and gave a quick nod of consent. 'Be as quick as you can,' Mrs Braithwaite said. 'We've a lot to get done before we see us beds tonight.'

Wiping her hot, sticky hands on her apron as she went, Amy scurried after her young mistress. But when they reached the door to Whiteladies' hall together, Amy hesitated. 'Miss Sophie, perhaps I'd better change my dress.'

'Stuff and nonsense! There's no time. This is an absolute emergency!' Swinging open the heavy oak door, Sophie swept up the wide staircase and along the landing to her room. 'Sit down, Amy, and I'll tell you all about it.'

'I don't think I'd better, miss,' protested Amy quietly. She was hot and dishevelled; wisps of damp hair clung to her neck and temples, and her cheeks were red and shiny from the kitchen's heat. 'I'm not allowed up here in my kitchen clothes, and anyway I'm sticky from the jam-making.'

'Ah yes, I see what you mean,' conceded Sophie. 'Very well, go and tidy yourself — but don't dawdle!'

After hurriedly washing her face, combing her hair and changing into her upstairs dress, Amy breathlessly returned to find Sophie staring disconsolately at an assortment of dresses, skirts and bodices strewn across her bed. 'I don't have a single, solitary thing remotely suitable!' she exclaimed without turning around. 'I'd really like to wear this new skirt, but all of the bodices look so dreary with it. What do you think?'

Amy considered the beautiful full skirt with its cream-and-brown woven stripes radiating from the broad waistband, and the array of bodices tossed higgledy-piggledy all around it. 'This high-necked one with the full sleeves would look good with the skirt, and the buttermilk shade matches the brown and cream nicely.'

'Yes, but it'll be a fearfully dull outfit, and this is such a special occasion,' responded Sophie plaintively. 'Clemmie and I have been invited by Amelia Deane and her brother Laurence to a garden party at Rufford. Amelia always dresses exquisitely — the absolute height of fashion; and although she's the most awful person, I just *have* to be at that garden party! You see, I really do like Laurence Deane, and I'm desperate to make a striking impression upon him.'

'I'm sure — '

'I was telling Clemmie how unbearably dreary all my clothes are,' went on Sophie. 'She said perhaps you could embellish them with your beautiful embroidery. You *can* do something, can't you? Oh, do say you can, Amy! I can't bear to look drab and sensible at the garden party. I want Laurence to find me pretty and utterly captivating.'

Amy chewed her lip, smoothing her fingertips over the delicate fabric of the buttermilk bodice. She sewed well, but she'd never attempted anything so ambitious. One mistake and the lovely garment would be ruined.

'I could embroider a floral spray on the left side, perhaps. With some fine beading — there are some beautiful little crystals in the sewing box . . . and the floral pattern could be repeated in tiny garlands upon the cuffs and high collar.' Amy raised her eyes hesitantly to Sophie's eager face. 'If you think that might be suitable, miss?'

'Perfect! I can see it already!' She beamed, pressing her palms together in sheer delight. 'Will you make some matching flowers to trim my bonnet?'

'I've never made flowers, miss.'

'Oh, I'm sure you'll manage wonderfully. The garden party's only a few days away, so you must begin straight away.' Sophie paused at a quiet tapping upon her door. 'Come!'

'Sophie, are you — ' Gilbert Paslew stood on the threshold, breaking off as his astonished gaze swept the room. 'Has a whirlwind passed this way, or did you simply decide to throw your clothes about for the sheer exhilaration of it?'

'I didn't have anything to wear for the garden party,' she lamented. 'Amy's come to my rescue! She's going to make me look so beautiful that Laurence Deane will find me utterly irresistible!'

'Got a magic wand, has she?' His gaze slid in Amy's direction, and she saw that his grey eyes were twinkling. 'And a large book of spells?'

'Beast!' Sophie bundled up a mauve jacket and hurled it at her older brother. 'It's terribly important that everything goes perfectly. I intend inviting the Deanes to Whiteladies during the summer, and since it's Amelia who decides which invitations they accept, I'm relying on you to win her over. It's up to you to ensure Amelia can't wait to visit us at Whiteladies.'

'Why me? Why can't Nicholas win her over?'

'Because Nick will be accompanying Clemmie, and besides, you're my brother.

You're supposed to help me. This garden party is my first opportunity to get to know Laurence Deane, and I need you to spirit Amelia away and keep her occupied for the afternoon.'

'So that you may ply your wiles on an unsuspecting Laurence?'

'Yes. No! Oh, I do so like him, Gilbert, but you know how quiet and shy Laurence Deane is.'

'He's probably not quiet at all,' returned Gilbert, leaning a shoulder against the door jamb. 'The poor blighter just never gets the chance to open his mouth with a sister like Amelia.'

'All the more reason for you to help me!' implored Sophie. 'Sweep her off her feet. Use your charm, for goodness sake!'

'I doubt charm will be effective where Amelia Deane is concerned,' commented Gilbert sceptically, catching Amy's eye once more. 'A scold's bridle is more suited to the task.'

Amy was following the discourse with increasing agitation. She could not leave the room without being dismissed, yet time was racing away, and with every passing minute Mrs Braithwaite would be more and more vexed by her absence.

'Don't be mean,' Sophie said to her brother.

'I'll do my best,' he answered quietly. 'Laurence is a decent chap, and he deserves to meet a nice, gentle woman. Meanwhile, I daresay he'll have to make do with you. Now, don't you think you've taken up enough of Amy's valuable time?'

'What?' Sophie turned to Amy, her face blank. 'Oh, I'd quite forgotten you were still here. Yes, you may go back to the kitchen, but put away these clothes first.' She strode to the door, following her brother onto the landing. 'Remember, I must have the bodice and flowers before Friday!'

Their voices disappeared down the staircase, and Amy began gathering up the strewn clothes. Most would need a good pressing before they were returned to the wardrobes. There were hours of extra work here. With sinking spirits, Amy raced down the backstairs to face the sharp edge of Mrs Braithwaite's tongue.

* * *

It was indeed very late when Amy finally hung up her apron at Whiteladies Grange and sped through Friars Wood into the lane towards the school-house. She wasn't surprised to find the small dwelling built into the school's side wall completely in darkness, nor to read the note pinned upon the low door. When Amy hadn't returned from Whiteladies by a given hour, Aunt Anne had taken Vicky home, where she would prepare supper for the family at Clockmakers Cottage and also put Vicky to bed, if necessary. Amy sighed with weariness and gratitude.

It had been a long, fraught day and exhaustion suddenly got the better of her. Sinking onto the cold stone doorstep, she rested her head in her hands. All she wanted was to get home and fall into her bed, but she really did need to speak to Dan Ainsworth without delay. Getting to her feet once more, she started into town and onto Abbotsgate, towards the Mermaid Inn.

Once there, she hesitated, uneasy about entering at this late hour. Hurrying through the archway into the stable yard, she tapped at the side door and waited patiently. When Ned Yarkin finally opened up, she was greatly relieved to see a familiar face.

'Good evening, Mr Yarkin. Could I see Dan, please?'

'Ye's out late, lass.' The elderly pot-man smiled at her through rheumy eyes. 'I'll fetch him out for ye.'

His footsteps shuffled away, and presently Dan emerged from the dark passageway. 'This is a nice surprise!'

'Can I ask you about something, Dan?'

'Course. Come in.'

'It's private.'

'Stables, then.' He reached for her arm and started across the shadowy yard. 'The cobbles are uneven, so mind your step. Here we are.' Closing the large doors behind them, Dan led the way inside. Lighting a lantern and hanging it upon a harness hook, he indicated a straw bale for Amy, and sat himself on the rungs of the loft ladder. 'Is it all right if the horses hear whatever you have to say?'

Amy smiled in spite of her fatigue; several of the well-groomed horses were glancing around from their stalls to consider her with large, shining brown eyes. 'Mrs Braithwaite and Mr Dobson were talking about a man who was attacked and robbed last market night,' she said, facing Dan in the flickering lantern light and somehow already beginning to feel better. 'She said you'd wanted to talk to him, but he'd already left on the coach.'

'Pawned his ring to pay the fare. It struck me as odd that the thief didn't take Wallace's ring and horse as well as his money — both'd be worth a fair bit,' commented Dan reflectively. 'Mind, there's quite a few things don't square up right. Wallace knew I was looking for him, and I had the notion he kept giving me the slip because he didn't want to talk too much about what happened that night. He boarded the Liverpool coach quick as snap, and I lost my chance. Pity, too. It would've made a grand story.'

Amy shook her head, not understanding. 'What do you mean?'

'It's the closest to proper news we've had in Monks Quay for a fair while, and the mystery about the ring and the horse not being taken make it all the more interesting. I wrote to the editor of the *Lancashire Clarion* months ago, and he said if I sent in a report of local news he'd gladly read it. But Sydney Wallace left for Liverpool before I could pin him down and get some proper details.'

'You were going to write about this in a newspaper?' She stared at him, aghast.

'Amy, I want to be a newspaperman!' he exclaimed. 'The *Clarion* might not be *The Times* or *The Glasgow Herald*, but it would've been a start.'

'It's wrong, Dan!' Amy cried. 'To even think about telling the whole of Lancashire about this — '

'Because Rory might be the robber?' he cut in. 'That's what you're thinking, isn't it? That Rory did it, and if I'd written about it in the *Clarion*, other folk besides you and me might start thinking the same?'

'No! Rory wouldn't — ' But the denial died on her lips.

'Wouldn't he?' demanded Dan harshly. 'I know what *I* think, but that's no matter.'

Amy clasped her hands tightly in her lap, unable to raise her eyes and meet Dan's clear gaze as taut silence lengthened between them.

'What *do* you think?' she mumbled at last. 'I don't know what to believe anymore, Dan! Pa heard Rory had been brawling in town that night. We did find him there the next morning, didn't we?'

'Huh! Rory was up to a sight more

that night than scrapping over the Tanners Row girls,' returned Dan briskly. 'Sydney Wallace was in the Mermaid early on. He had his meal and played some cards. Then I saw him and Theodore Buxton sitting in the back room with their heads together, and Buxton wasn't looking any too pleased. I don't know when Wallace left, but after Rory came in and lost all his money, he and Buxton were in a huddle over a couple of tots. Then Rory was gone, and a few hours later Wallace was attacked on the drover's road.'

Amy ran her tongue over dry lips. Theodore Buxton again!

'I've poked around town. Asked a few questions. I've no proof of what happened. It's just my opinion.'

She swallowed hard, her heart hammering. 'Tell me.'

'I reckon there was dealings between Buxton and Sydney Wallace, but it turned sour and Buxton sent Rory after him,' continued Dan evenly. 'Wallace wasn't fit enough or young enough to

101

put up a fight. Rory stole his money right enough, but left the ring and probably rode the horse back to the Green Man before turning it loose. He had a few more drinks, ended up in Tanners Row, and the rest we know.'

'I can't believe you were going to print all this in a newspaper just to — to feed your ambitions!' Amy rose unsteadily, her eyes sparkling. 'It's despicable, Dan. How could you?'

Crossing the stable in a couple of strides, Dan was before her as she turned to leave. 'Ask yourself a question, Amy. Why are you angry I wanted to write about this?' he demanded coldly. 'Then face up to the answer. Because, like me, you believe it was your brother who robbed Sydney Wallace and left him for dead on the drover's road!'

4

The bells of All Hallows were ringing out on Sunday morning as the Macfarlenes walked across the meadow to services. 'I recall telling your ma that if I was ashore all the while, I'd like to ring the bells,' remarked Ramsay, helping Vicky clamber over the stile. 'I always fancied myself as a bell-ringer.'

'I didn't know that!' exclaimed Amy, who'd never thought her father in the least musical. 'You've never mentioned bell-ringing before!'

'Oh, aye. It's in the blood. My father rang bells in the pit town where he was born, just as his father did before him. Then when Father left Scotland for the mines on the Isle of Man, he rang at his local kirk. I had a go myself as a lad in Laxey.'

'Perhaps I'd better start ringing,' said Edmund with a smile. 'Keep the custom in the family.'

'If bell-ringing's to be kept in *this* family, it'll have to be you who does it,' said Ramsay wryly. 'I somehow can't see Rory ringing bells. We were lucky he came to church for his sister's wedding! Though to be fair to the lad,' he went on seriously, 'he's shaped up a fair bit since I came ashore. Hasn't stayed out late or gone drinking up at the Green Man. All credit to him if he's mended his ways and is working hard, but Rory's got the ability to do a lot better for himself than Paslew's clay pits.'

Amy's heart ached at meeting Pa's earnest eyes, understanding how deeply he wanted to believe the best and be proud of his eldest son. Vicky was skipping ahead of them, and Edmund was talking to Pa about helping lift potatoes at Barraclough's farm ready for when the *Jenet Rae* sailed; but so wrapped up was she in her own sombre thoughts, that Amy scarcely heard a word.

When they reached All Hallows, Edmund strode across to meet Nicholas Buxton, who was just arriving in the Paslews' carriage, while the others went on inside. Taking her place in the choir stalls, Amy watched absently as Pa and Vicky settled into their usual pew. Vicky immediately spotted one of her new school friends and waved wildly to a red-haired little girl in a gingham pinafore. She'd taken to school like a duck to water, and it was lovely to see her so happy and excited.

Amy breathed in deeply the calming atmosphere of the Norman church with its whitewashed walls and brilliantly coloured windows. Aunt Anne nodded in Amy's direction as she passed by, speaking quietly with Reverend Linley as she sat at the organ and unfolded her music. Not many folk in Monks Quay could play the organ, and those who could took turns at playing for services.

The church was filling as the congregation gradually filed in. Among the last to enter were the Paslews. Mr and Mrs Paslew and their daughters led the way to their family pew near the lady chapel, and Amy caught herself wondering if Miss Sophie had been pleased with the buttermilk bodice and bonnet flowers she'd spent so many painstaking hours on. After studying the Paslew sisters for a minute or two, she decided Sophie looked particularly animated, so perhaps the outfit, the garden party at Rufford and the bid to impress her young man had been successful.

Amy's gaze drifted once more to the west door, where the last few parishioners were hurrying inside. Gilbert Paslew, Nicholas Buxton and Teddy were bringing up the rear, exchanging a final few words before going their separate ways. With a pang, Amy realised she was looking out for Dan Ainsworth. His parents and younger brothers were seated a few rows behind the Macfarlenes, but Dan was not with them. Amy chided herself for feeling so very disappointed not to see him, for Dan rarely came to church except at Christmas. She scarcely noticed Gilbert Paslew slipping unobtrusively into the back row of the choir stalls before the music swelled beneath Aunt Anne's deft fingertips. Reverend Linley stepped up into the pulpit and All Hallows' Sunday service commenced.

* * *

'You all go on ahead; I want to catch up with Harry Smedley,' Ramsay was saying as they left the church, nodding to where the miller and his family were climbing up onto their cart. 'I'll see you back at Clockmakers.'

'Very well, Pa.' Amy paused, waiting for Edmund to join them. He was once more deep in conversation with Nicholas Buxton and Gilbert Paslew.

'Edmund's become very friendly with Nicholas, hasn't he?' observed Anne. 'I must say, Nicholas seems a thoroughly nice, considerate person. Quite a different character from his elder — ' She broke off as the three young men came within hearing and joined them upon the path leading down to the lichgate.

'Aunt Anne, Gilbert's offered to give

me some of his books for my scholarship work!' Edmund enthused. 'He has all the Greek ones you said I should study.'

'That's thoughtful of you, Gilbert.' Anne nodded in approval at her former pupil. 'It will be of enormous help for Edmund to have access to those texts.'

'Books should be read and used and discussed, Miss Shawcross — you taught me that a long time ago,' he returned with a warm smile. 'It's very rewarding to pass them on to somebody like Edmund, who is genuinely interested in all they have to say.'

'My nephew has a sharp intellect and we have great hopes for his future,' she replied, adding, 'I was pleased to hear you singing in the choir again, Gilbert. We need a good, strong tenor. May I assume you're intending to stay in Monks Quay?'

'Yes. Uncle William and I have been talking at length this summer — about the choir and a great deal more besides. You see, during my last year at Oxford I was seriously considering the priesthood, but I'm still not certain I have a true vocation.' Gilbert added drily, 'Of course, my father is delighted I've finally seen sense and am returning to Monks Quay to join the family business.'

'Hardly surprising,' commented Anne crisply. 'You are his only son and heir. May I add your name to the organ-playing rota?'

'Please do. Although I'm frightfully rusty and will need hours of practice before I'm fit for the ears of the congregation.' He made to take his leave, pausing to smile at Amy. 'I understand you were responsible for gathering and arranging the flowers this week, Miss Macfarlene? The church looked especially beautiful today.'

'Thank you,' Amy murmured, warm colour rising to her cheeks as Gilbert Paslew held her gaze. Then the moment was broken, and raising his hat and bidding them all a friendly good day, he strode across the churchyard towards the bridle path leading to Whiteladies Grange.

'Amy, I won't be in for dinner,' said Edmund cheerfully. 'Nicholas and I are borrowing Dan Ainsworth's boat and sailing out to Fiddlers Pike and back this afternoon.'

'Dan?' echoed Amy blankly. 'You've seen Dan?'

'Of course! Since I've been lifting potatoes out at Barraclough's farm, I see Dan all the time when I'm going through town.' Edmund gave her a cheery wave as he and Nicholas started away up the coast toward the boathouses. 'See you later!'

'Enjoy yourselves!' she called after them. 'Be careful — mind the sand banks and keep well clear of Judas Rocks!'

With Vicky running on ahead, Amy fell into step beside Aunt Anne as they strolled across the meadows away from All Hallows. Amy hadn't seen Dan since that night in the stable, yet he'd rarely been absent from her thoughts. Although they hadn't actually quarrelled, she no longer felt able to simply go to the Mermaid Inn and see him. If only it were possible for her to bump into Dan as casually and often as Teddy evidently did. Aunt Anne's voice jarred Amy from her reverie.

'I wonder what your father wanted with Harry Smedley?' pondered Anne, tightening the ribbons of her bonnet against the freshening breeze as the sea and Clockmakers Cottage slid into sight. 'Ah well, I daresay we'll find out in due course.'

* * *

Rory had still been sleeping when the family left for church. Now upon their return, he was nowhere to be found. With dinner cooking nicely, Aunt Anne and Vicky out gathering gooseberries for the rice pudding they'd have at teatime before Pa sailed, and Pa himself not yet back from his talk with Harry Smedley, Amy went upstairs to tidy her brothers' room and make their beds. Gathering together the dirty washing, she emptied the pockets before taking the garments down to the tub and almost cried out when, turning from the task, she found Rory standing behind her.

'Well, well, little sister!' He grinned, but there was scant humour in his countenance. 'Looking for something?'

She faced him squarely, and in that instant was utterly convinced that proof or no proof, Dan Ainsworth had been absolutely right.

'If you're looking for a purse of sovereigns to give back to their proper owner,' he sneered, 'you'll not find 'em here!'

'It was you, wasn't it?' she challenged, her gaze steady. 'You attacked and robbed Sydney Wallace!'

'Sydney Wallace?' echoed Rory wryly. 'Who's he when he's at home?'

'Could you really have wanted money so badly that you'd do something so wicked?'

'Don't come over all holier-than-thou, Amy. You're so wrapped up in your own cosy little world that you've no idea what life is really like,' he retaliated bitterly. 'Wallace was working for a friend of mine, but he got greedy and started taking a slice of the profits. I did this friend a favour by teaching Wallace a lesson he won't forget — and made a pretty penny or two into the bargain.'

'And now you're in league with Theodore Buxton!'

'Is that a fact?' he taunted, his grin widening. 'I'm not fretting you'll shop me. Nor will Dan Ainsworth. He could, but he won't, because of you. Poor beggar's smitten! No, if you were going to turn me in or tell Pa, you'd have already done it. You're soft, Amy. Now you and your conscience will have to live with what you've found out.'

'It's not too late to mend your ways,' she implored. 'You can never put right what you did to Sydney Wallace, but you don't have to continue with what-ever schemes you and Theodore Buxton are plotting. It'll break Pa's heart if he ever learns the truth. You must stop, Rory. Stop now, please!'

'Stop! Stop!' he mocked, watching Amy's horrified expression as he slid the pistol from the pocket of his coat, extending his palm so she might see it more closely. 'Why, me and this little beauty haven't even started yet!'

Time hung in suspension. Amy could only stare at the deadly weapon as brother and sister stood perfectly motionless in the still room. The rattle of the front gate finally broke the heavy silence, and Rory returned the pistol to his pocket. 'Do I hear the family returning?' He arched an eyebrow, stepping aside so Amy might quit the room ahead of him. 'Let's go down and eat dinner, shall we?'

Amy didn't taste a mouthful of the delicious meal she'd cooked for the family, nor hear a word of conversation, despite this being Pa's last few hours at home before sailing with the potato crop to the Isle of Man. As soon as she and Aunt Anne started clearing the table, Rory scraped back his chair.

'Before you go dashing off, son,' said Ramsay, 'I want to talk to you.'

'I've things to do.'

'I daresay, but this'll not take long,' Ramsay replied mildly. 'Sit down, lad. It's important.'

Shrugging, Rory sat and folded his arms upon the table. 'What's up this time?'

Amy and her aunt exchanged glances. Setting down a pile of crockery upon the board, Anne crossed to the step where Vicky was playing with her rag doll. 'Shall we collect some gooseberries for tea?'

Vicky's face crumpled into a frown. 'But we've already picked lots of berries today.'

'You can never have too many gooseberries with a rice pudding,' replied Anne, firmly ushering the child outdoors. 'That's what I always say.'

'Son, I've had a talk with Harry Smedley,' said Ramsay, and Amy could hear the pride in her father's quiet voice and see the light in his eyes as he looked across the table at his eldest son. 'His mill's prospering, and the packet's carrying more and more of Smedley's flour with every year that goes by.

Harry needs another strong lad up at the mill, and he's willing to take you on. You start tomorrow morning — '

'Hang on, I've had enough of this!' cut in Rory, shaking his head in disbelief. 'You went cap in hand to Harry Smedley and got me a job without a word to me? Smedley knows what he can do with his milling, for I want no part of it!'

'Rory, don't be hasty! I only want what's best for you, son!' persisted Ramsay earnestly. 'You'll be set up for life once you've a proper trade to your name. You can maybe go into business for yourself one day. It's a grand opportunity!'

'When will you get it, Pa? I'm done bowing and scraping to the likes of Paslew and Harry Smedley,' declared Rory, snatching his coat from the chair-back. 'I've got plans — plans as'll take me far away from Monks Quay! I'm off into town. I'll not see you again before you sail with the tide.' Pulling on his coat, Rory paused at the threshold. His anger and resentment suddenly seemed to subside, and he briefly met Ramsay's gaze before turning away. 'Have a safe trip, Pa.'

★   ★   ★

Standing at the quayside that evening, Amy longed to comfort her father before he sailed. However, she no more had words to do so now than earlier that afternoon, when Rory had gone from Clockmakers and left her and Pa alone in the quiet cottage.

'Do you *have* to go away?' Vicky was saying, clutching Ramsay's calloused hand tightly. 'I don't want you to go!'

'*I* don't want me to go,' he laughed, swinging her up into his arms. As he hugged the little girl, Amy noticed his gaze travelling along the quayside and up towards the town. Poor Pa — he was still hoping Rory would relent and come to bid him farewell.

'Ted, you've grown up all of a sudden, and I'm right proud of you,' said Ramsay thickly, shaking Edmund's

117

hand and then impulsively wrapping his arms about the boy's narrow shoulders. 'You did a man's job lifting those spuds for Barraclough — the *Jenet Rae* couldn't have sailed without 'em.' Turning to Amy, he smiled down at her. 'You're your ma's daughter and no mistake! Take care of your brothers and sister for me, lass.'

'I will, Pa. Don't worry, about anything. Just come home safe.'

With a final wave from the deck, the *Jenet Rae*, laden with her cargo of potatoes and grain and riding low in the water, set sail and was borne away on the tide. A lump leapt to Amy's throat. Pa was gone, and she'd never felt so alone.

★   ★   ★

When Amy came down from putting Vicky to bed that night, Edmund glanced up from his reading. It was the first opportunity they'd had to talk. 'Did Pa and Rory have another row

118

today?' he asked.

'Not really. Why?'

Edmund didn't answer at once. 'I think Rory's gone.'

Alarm and fear gripped Amy. 'Whatever do you mean?'

'I may be mistaken,' he went on hastily, 'but when I was in our room earlier, I noticed that although his work clothes and boots are still there, his razor and other bits and pieces weren't on his shelf.'

'Rory said he had plans.' Expelling a slow breath, Amy sank down at the table. 'But to just up and go without a word . . . '

'We'll manage without him,' responded Edmund firmly. 'You, Vicky and me. Don't worry, Amy. It'll be all right, you'll see.'

Presently she left Edmund to his studies and stepped out into the gathering dusk. Ragged clouds were drifting across the night sky, and she walked briskly along the hard, damp sand towards one of her favourite haunts. Clambering up onto the smooth, time-worn hogsback rock, she sat and stared far away into the blackness of the distant sea. Pa and the *Jenet Rae* were out there somewhere. He and his crew had worked hard to make good what repairs they could, but what if their efforts were not enough? Amy was overwhelmed with foreboding. What if the packet got into difficulties, as Pa said she might? Suppose — ? Amy squeezed closed her eyes, as though to shut out her thoughts.

'Amy!' The low voice came to her from the dark. 'It's only me.'

'Dan!' she gasped, tearful at the sudden happiness she felt from just seeing him.

'I knocked at Clockmakers, and when Edmund said you'd gone for a walk, I thought I might find you here at the hogs.'

'I'm so glad to see you, Dan. I'm very sorry for making such a fuss about the newspaper story. Of course you should've written it.'

'I spoke a fair bit out of turn myself that night.' He smiled, sitting down on the rounded hogsback beside her. 'Did your da get away all right?'

She nodded, her gaze once more drawn out to the vast emptiness of the sea. Suddenly, Amy could keep her silence no longer. She *had* to tell someone, and Dan was the only person in whom she could confide.

'Rory's gone, Dan! Gone for good, I think. He *did* attack Mr Wallace on the drover's road.' She poured out the whole story: the clandestine meetings she'd witnessed at All Hallows and the resting place, the package, the pistol, everything.

'You shouldn't have kept this to yourself,' he murmured when Amy's tale was done. 'You can always tell me anything. You know that.'

'Yes,' she mumbled. Unexpected emotion was welling deep within her and she looked away quickly, sudden tears stinging her eyes.

'There, there, lass,' he comforted her, tentatively reaching an arm about her trembling shoulders. Gently drawing her closer, he rested his cheek against the softness of her hair. 'I'm here for you, Amy. And here I'll be for as long as ever you want me.'

5

Although what little breeze there was blew away from Amy as she stood on the drying green at Whiteladies Grange beating carpets, she felt grimy and covered in dust from head to toe. Her raised arms were aching from hours of wielding the large wooden beater, though her thoughts were far from the chore of cleaning the drawing-room carpets. In her mind's eye, she was rereading Fanny's latest letter which had arrived earlier that day with the coach from York.

The months are passing so swiftly, Fanny had written in her beautiful formal hand. *It already seems a lifetime ago that I was with you all at Clockmakers Cottage. Our honeymoon trip to Pemberley is now but a distant memory, and we are thoroughly installed* here in our home at Carteret Square.

While the house is not perhaps as large as I had imagined, it is beautifully proportioned, with spacious rooms, splendid high ceilings and the most impressive fireplaces you've ever seen! Oh, I do wish you could see it all, Amy. Every room is furnished so tastefully, and everything is so fine and comfortable. My new home is even more than I ever dreamed a house could be!

We haven't yet entertained, however I am planning my first ever dinner party. I am at once excited and fearfully apprehensive! From working at Whiteladies Grange, you have some notion of the manner in which people of quality do things. I have no such experience and am anxious about making mistakes and disappointing and embarrassing Theo.

I shall have another new gown for the dinner party; Theo insists upon it. He is the most dear and generous husband imaginable. I scarcely would have thought *it possible to be so happy, and I hope you marry as well and wisely as I have! How is Dan Ainsworth, by the way?* Amy could picture her sister's arch smile as she wrote those words. *Good men are hard to find. Don't let Dan get away!*

Carteret Square is within sight of the minster, and when Theo is away from home on matters of business, it is a very pleasant stroll for me to attend evensong. Theo, alas, is not a church-goer, so we don't attend services together. Now we are firmly established in York, Theo is always so very busy, and I fear his absences upon business will become more frequent. After the bustle of Clockmakers Cottage, I confess to feeling very alone in this big house whenever he is gone. I'll welcome Nicholas's company when he returns from Whiteladies Grange. I don't suppose he'll accompany Theo on business trips. I can't envisage Nicholas as a shrewd man of commerce, can you?

Last week Theo and I went to the

ballet, and a few evenings before that to a production of Hamlet. Theo declared it 'sterling'! Wherever we go, we seem to bump into all manner of wealthy, important people, and Theo knows them all. I am so very proud to be his wife, and I still can't quite believe he chose me when he might so easily have wed the daughter of an influential family here in York.

This really is the most lively and fascinating place, Amy! Every day on my walks and drives I discover new sources of interest, and the shops are absolutely breath-taking! Oh, I meant to tell you something in my last letter and quite forgot. I thought I saw Rory, here in York!

Theo and I had arranged to meet for luncheon, but I was rather early so was browsing along Petergate. I'd stopped to look in the windows of a draper there, when a man came out from the coffee-house across the street — I particularly noticed because it was one of the coffee-houses Theo *frequents. At first glance I thought it was Rory, but he strode away so quickly I wasn't able to get a really good look at him. And besides, although the man I saw wasn't a gentleman, he appeared well-groomed and dressed smartly — quite unlike Rory.*

Finally finishing the carpet-beating, Amy dusted down her apron and dress with the flats of her hands before starting indoors. There was no doubt in her mind it *had* been Rory in York. Putting two and two together, wasn't it likely he'd been at the coffee-house — described by Fanny as one Theo visited often — to meet Theodore Buxton and discuss whatever dealings the pair had together? Deals that were apparently bringing prosperity to Rory.

Replacing the beater in the cupboard, Amy hurried along the passageway past the kitchen. Mrs Braithwaite was sharing a pot of tea with Edith Barraclough, who made the most of her regular trips up to Whiteladies with the eggs, butter and milk to share a sup and chat with her old friend.

'Amy!' called Edie Barraclough, glimpsing Amy from the corner of her eye as she passed the open doorway. 'If your Edmund wants more work up at t'farm, will you tell him Collie said he has only to knock on t'door and ask? There's usually summat for a hardworking lad to do around the place, and Collie's always on the lookout for somebody to take on the hay-run to Liverpool and back.'

'Thanks, Mrs Barraclough, but Teddy really needs to concentrate on his studies from now on. I don't want him working regularly.'

'Don't dally getting yourself cleaned up and presentable, girl,' commented Gladys Braithwaite sharply. 'There's fresh flowers needed upstairs.'

Washed and wearing her black dress and a clean apron, Amy took the trug and followed the paths meandering through the flower gardens. Selecting blooms suitable for the ladies' posy bowls and the crystal vases in the dining and drawing rooms, she could hear the murmur of voices from the south-facing terrace. Alfred and Gilbert Paslew were taking their coffee there, and apparently discussing the documents Alfred Paslew had spread out on the table before them.

An hour or so later, Amy was in the drawing-room arranging the flowers when Albert Paslew strode in, with his two younger daughters following.

'Absolutely not, Sophie!' Paslew noticed Amy, who immediately bobbed a curtsey to her master and made to quit the room. 'Stay where you are, girl. Carry on with what you're doing. Sophie, I refuse to squander money constructing an orangery just so you can impress your young man!'

'Laurence isn't my young man!' she protested, adding coyly, 'Not quite yet, anyway.'

'I'm sure he will be, if that's what you've decided upon,' commented Paslew, crossing to the writing desk and taking an inventory from the blotter.

'Please, Father!' persisted Sophie. 'An orangery would be so exquisite!'

'Exquisite and expensive, although not necessarily in that order,' he returned, running a shrewd eye down the list in his hands. 'I'm perfectly happy for you to have your weekends and your parties and whatever else here, providing I don't need to do more than greet your guests and be passably civil to them on the mercifully infrequent occasions I run into them. Anything more is quite out of the question.'

'Very well, Father,' replied Sophie meekly, elbowing her younger sister sharply in the ribs.

'Might we have new dresses?' piped up Clemmie dutifully. 'Particularly Sophie. It'd be dreadful if she was shown up by Laurence's sister!'

'Amelia has such flair,' chipped in Sophie.

'Amelia Deane has a father with more money than sense,' Paslew remarked, consulting his pocket watch with a frown. 'Ah, there you are, Gilbert! Ready to go? Good. I have the inventory, and you've amended the contract, haven't you?'

'Father!' Sophie pursued him from the drawing-room into the hall. 'May Clemmie and I go to Liverpool, and purchase a very few things?'

'You'll have to see your mother about it.' Taking his hat, Alfred Paslew strode to the front door.

Gilbert Paslew paused in the drawing-room, smiling across to Amy. 'More beautifully arranged flowers, Miss Macfarlene. These really are lovely!'

Before Amy could return his smile, Gilbert had followed Alfred Paslew through the hall and out to the waiting horses. While she finished the flowers, she watched father and son canter down the drive and take the northbound ride beyond the gates of Whiteladies Grange.

'Erm, Amy?'

She spun around to find Clemmie Paslew hovering behind her, and at once bobbed a curtsey.

'I-I'd like you to accept this.' Clemmie stepped forwards, stretching her hands out and offering Amy a neatly wrapped little box. 'It's, well, it's my way of thanking you for the runner. It was the nicest surprise. That corner of the garden is my special place, you see. Your embroidery depicted it beautifully.'

'Thank you, miss,' murmured Amy, quite taken aback. She glanced across at Clemmie, guessing they were about the same age. Clemmie Paslew was plump, rather plain, and she seemed very shy and unsure. Amy warmed to her at once. 'I love flowers and plants, and I love sewing too, so . . .' Her voice trailed off awkwardly, and both girls suddenly smiled at each other, the difference in their stations momentarily forgotten.

'I've wanted to give you something for ages!' exclaimed Clemmie. 'But I didn't have anything I thought you'd like. When I heard Gilbert was going to Liverpool on business for Father, I asked him to get these from Mosley's, the haberdasher in Bold Street. I do hope you like them.'

The little box, and her curiosity as to its contents, had been burning a hole in Amy's apron pocket all day long. However, with Mrs Braithwaite's eagle eye upon her every moment, she hadn't had any opportunity to open it up.

'You'll never guess what happened today at Whiteladies!' she said when Dan met her at the school-house that evening.

'Alfred Paslew promised to pay you a decent wage and give you a day off every week?'

'Better than that!' returned Amy blithely, beaming up at him. Dan had taken to seeing her each evening when she collected Vicky from Aunt Anne's, and it was the part of the day Amy looked forward to most of all. 'Miss Clemmie gave me a present!'

'What for?'

'She was pleased with some needlework I did,' said Amy, dipping into her pocket and withdrawing the box. Slowing her pace, she untied the string and unfolded the paper, lifting the lid of the small square box. 'Oh Dan, look! Aren't they beautiful?'

He looked down over her shoulder. 'It's a pair of scissors.'

'Proper sewing scissors!' exclaimed Amy, carefully taking the finely crafted swan-necked silver scissors into her hand. 'What a kind gift!'

'It's not hard to be kind when you've money like they've got.'

'Oh, you!' She laughed, shaking her head as they followed Vicky across the meadows towards Clockmakers Cottage. 'We had another letter from Fanny this morning. She's very happy and loves living in York, but she thought she saw Rory coming from a coffee-house near the minster. Do you think it was him, Dan? Fanny couldn't be certain.'

'Like as not it was,' he commented, his hand upon the cottage gate. 'I wonder what he and Theodore Buxton are up to? Nothing on t'right side of the law, that's for sure.'

'Are you coming in for a cup of tea?'

Amy asked, suddenly loath to see him go. 'Can you stay for supper?'

''Got to get back to the Mermaid. The coach from Preston'll be in within the hour.' He paused, holding her gaze for a long moment. 'I'd best be on my way. See you tomorrow, Amy.'

She nodded, watching him start back towards town before turning with a sigh and going indoors.

★   ★   ★

The meal was over and cleared, Vicky was in bed, and Amy was making the most of the day's light replacing buttons on Edmund's school shirt, her silver swan-necked scissors on the table beside her. Despite Dan's scornfulness, she felt a glow of happiness whenever her gaze rested upon them. What a kind and thoughtful girl Clemmie was!

The evening was closing in to dusk when the cottage gate creaked and the door knocker rattled quietly.

'Mr Paslew!' Amy exclaimed when

she saw who the visitor was.

'Gilbert, please! Good evening, Miss Macfarlene. Is Edmund at home? I promised I'd dig out some books about the Greek victory at Marathon.' His face broke into a broad smile and he indicated the weighty tomes in his arms. 'As you can see, I've done exactly that.'

'Teddy's outside chopping wood.' She smiled, stepping aside in welcome. 'Won't you come in?' Showing Gilbert a seat, she hastily cleared her sewing from the table.

'I see Clemmie gave you the scissors,' he observed with a smile.

'They're beautiful!' she responded. 'I understand you chose them. Thank you.'

'I was merely the messenger boy following strict instructions. Clemmie was touched at the care you'd taken with the runner you made for her.' Gilbert went on seriously, 'Although she doesn't say much, Clemmie does feel things deeply — unlike Sophie.' His grey eyes were all of a sudden mischievous. 'Who's unbelievably shallow and says rather a lot most of the time.'

Amy faltered a little self-consciously. 'I, er, I'll tell Teddy you're here.'

★ ★ ★

'Is this one, Amy?' called Vicky from across the vegetable patch they were weeding. 'Shall I pull it up?'

'Yes, but remember to pull gently, and try to get the root up instead of snapping it off at the stem.' She sat back on her heels, pushing her sun bonnet from her damp forehead as Edmund sauntered into the garden, grinning from ear to ear. 'How did you get on at Whiteladies — or needn't I ask?'

'Gilbert asked me lots of questions about the books he lent me, and we discussed all sorts of things. He really listened to what I had to say, Amy. As if my opinions were worthy.' Edmund added exuberantly, 'He said the paper I'd written on Virgil was already of a high standard, and if I go on working hard I'll have an excellent chance of gaining the scholarship!'

'Well done, Teddy!' Amy got to her feet, hugging him hard. 'That's wonderful!'

'He's lent me another batch of books and set me more exercises. I said we'd have our next meeting here. That was all right, wasn't it? Only, I felt a bit queer being up at Whiteladies Grange,' he owned, adding, 'I mean, it was all very nice, and Gilbert introduced me to his sister, and she was really nice.'

'That'd be Miss Clemmie,' said Amy with a smile, bending to cut some beans for dinner. 'Yes, of course you must bring Mr Gilbert here for your discussions. You can take him into the sitting-room. You won't be disturbed there.'

'I met Mr Paslew, too — the one who owns the *Jenet Rae*. He was very polite, but I'm sure he thought Gilbert should be doing something more important with his time than helping me with my studies.'

'From what I've heard,' remarked Amy drily, 'Alfred Paslew regards anything not connected to making money as a waste of time.'

'I suppose so, but he wasn't at all the tyrant Rory and lots of other people paint him as.'

'You were a guest in his home, Teddy,' she replied mildly. 'I daresay other folk see Mr Paslew in a very different light.'

'Perhaps you're right.' He paused, savouring the moment. 'I've something else to tell you, Amy. After I'd seen Gilbert, Nicholas and I went into town, and — well, just come inside and I'll show you!'

Amy and Vicky hurried indoors after him, and there in the centre of the table were a small blue glass brooch shaped like a star, a rag doll, and a little pile of coins.

'This is for you.' He gave Vicky the doll and she at once raced out into the garden with it. 'The brooch is yours, Amy. It reminded me of the Dog Star tale you tell Vicky when Pa's away. And the money's for you, too. For the family, you know.'

Amy swallowed hard, tears springing to her eyes as she touched the blue glass brooch with her fingertips. 'I don't understand.'

'Working on Collie Barraclough's farm now and then is all right, but I've been on the lookout for a more regular job.' Edmund's smooth face was bright with excitement. 'Dan Ainsworth's taken me on to help in the stables at the Mermaid! This is my first week's wages — in advance, because Dan reckons he can trust me.'

'Teddy, you can't do this!' exclaimed Amy. 'I appreciate it, but I told you when you wanted to help at Barraclough's that it could only be temporary.'

'I know what you told me, Amy, but I don't agree!' he returned hotly. 'I've proved I can do a day's work, and now I want a proper job!'

'Cleaning out the stalls at the Mermaid Inn?'

'What's wrong with that? Pa would say it's honest work.'

'Yes, I know he would. And it is,' she

said, managing to keep her voice even despite her growing anger. 'It isn't the job, Teddy — it's you! I don't want you working for pennies when you should be studying for your future.'

'What about what *I* want?' he demanded. 'I told Aunt Anne about it on my way from town and she thought it an admirable idea! She said I'll make far better progress studying on my own away from school now Gilbert's helping and lending me the best books. Aunt Anne is even drawing up a timetable for me to follow. Everything will work out, you'll see!'

'No, Teddy.' She shook her head sadly. 'I understand you're disappointed, but it's for the best.'

'Best for whom?' he retorted stubbornly. 'If I want to get a job, I shall!'

'Why can't you see how foolish it is to jeopardise your scholarship for a job in the Mermaid's stables?' she persisted in exasperation. 'I won't allow you to do it, Teddy!'

'You can't stop me!' Snatching up his

books and writing tablet, Edmund stormed from the cottage.

Amy made to follow him into the garden, then stopped in her tracks. Perhaps it would be wiser to give him a little time alone. Teddy was sure to see the sense of her decision as soon as he calmed down. With a sigh, she picked up the pretty little brooch. Resting it upon her palm, the clear blue glass caught the sunlight so it sparkled and glinted like a real star. Dear Teddy! How like him to be so unselfish, but it really wouldn't do.

Ruefully, she gathered up the scattered coins from the table and with a glance to the garden, where Edmund was studying and Vicky playing with her new doll, Amy slipped away from Clockmakers Cottage.

She found Dan Ainsworth in the stables, repairing a bridle in a corner of the airy, sunlit room next to the stalls. It was quiet in there, and smelled of linseed, beeswax and sweet summer hay. He glanced up in surprise when she walked in.

'Teddy's wages,' she said softly, setting down the coins upon the workbench. 'I'm sorry there's some missing. He purchased gifts for Vicky and me before he brought the money home. I'll make up the difference next week, when I'm paid at Whiteladies.'

Dan raised his eyes to search Amy's solemn face. 'What's all this about?'

'I wish you hadn't offered Teddy that job!' she burst out in dismay. 'I daresay you meant well — '

'I'm obliged for that small consideration!' he cut in sarcastically.

'Please don't be difficult, Dan! I've had a row with Teddy, and all this unpleasantness could have been avoided if only you'd asked me about the stables job first!'

His stony gaze held hers. 'Why, exactly, would I do that?'

'Because you know I don't want Teddy working!' she exclaimed impatiently. 'It's out of the question. He needs to concentrate on preparing for his scholarship examination.'

'You need to get your facts straight, Amy. I didn't offer Edmund the job — although happen I would've, if I'd thought on it. He saw it chalked up on the board. Of the lads who came in and asked, Edmund was the best, so he got the job.'

'Teddy saw the chance to earn some money. He doesn't realise his whole future is at stake!' she retorted angrily. 'For goodness sake, he's just a boy, Dan!'

'You don't give Edmund the credit he's due, do you?' returned Dan coldly. 'He's young, but there're lads his age and younger at the clay pits. Besides, Edmund's more of a man in his ways and how he thinks than plenty who are much older. Your other brother Rory being a prime example.'

'Can't you understand — '

'It's *you* as doesn't understand!' he cut in harshly. 'You don't want Edmund to get a job, so you knock him down and come running to me behind his back to return his wages! You're wrong, Amy! Dead wrong. If you'd set out to humiliate Edmund and rob the lad of his pride and self-respect, you couldn't have done it any better!'

Amy stared into his accusing eyes, anger and frustration draining from her. The stables were very quiet, yet the snuffle and whicker of horses, the rustling of dry hay and the soft whirr of swallows' wings as they flew amongst the beams high in the loft were loud to her ears. 'I hadn't . . . didn't think about it. How it must seem from Teddy's point of view,' she mumbled unhappily, lowering her eyes from the keen scrutiny of Dan's gaze. 'I wouldn't hurt Teddy for the world.'

'I know that, and so does he,' said Dan softly, going to her as she stood forlornly in a shaft of sunshine filtering through the dusty glass panes. 'You try too hard, lass. Always thinking about what's best for others.'

'Dan . . . '

'Happen it's time you started thinking about yourself, Amy,' he murmured, gently drawing her close and lowering his lips to hers. 'About what *you* want.'

Hours later, after Amy's apologies were made and all was well again with Teddy, she was alone at Clockmakers Cottage polishing Ma's piano. While she worked, her thoughts brimmed with the sound of Dan Ainsworth's voice, the remembrance of his strong face gazing down at her, and the warm pressure of his lips upon her own.

⋆　⋆　⋆

Gladys Braithwaite bustled into the kitchen after discussing the day's menus with Mrs Paslew upstairs. 'Huh, seems they want a fancy dinner for tomorrow night — special guests!' she huffed. 'A bit more notice wouldn't have come amiss! Amy, make yourself presentable. The missus is waiting for you in the drawing-room.'

'Why?' Amy spun around from the sink. 'Is something wrong?'

'How should I know? I'm not a

mind-reader, am I?' The cook double-tied an apron about her ample middle. 'Look sharp, girl! The missus'll not like being kept waiting.'

Eleanor Paslew was seated at the writing desk beside the window. 'Amy! Come in.' She looked up from the letter in her hands. 'My daughters are going to Liverpool on Thursday to shop and visit their dressmaker. They'll be putting up overnight and returning on the midday coach. I'd like you to accompany them.'

'Y-yes, ma'am.' Amy's thoughts were racing. Liverpool! She'd never been away from Monks Quay before! Would Aunt Anne be able to stay at Clockmakers Cottage and care for Edmund and Vicky while she was gone? 'Thank you, ma'am.'

'I want you to do some shopping for me. I've made out a list. Most of the establishments are in Bold Street, so you shouldn't have any difficulty finding them. I had intended making the trip myself, however we have guests coming to stay and I'm needed at Whiteladies. There's something else, too.' Mrs Paslew smiled, and it seemed to Amy her whole face lit up with happiness. 'Our eldest daughter and her husband have written to tell us we are to be grandparents for the first time! The baby won't arrive for some months, however I want you to make a complete set of everything an infant requires, and you must embroider it as beautifully as you did Clemmie's runner.'

'Yes, ma'am. But, that is . . . ' said Amy, chewing her lip. ' . . . I knew Miss Clemmie, ma'am! At least, I knew she was fond of the walled garden, so I put that on her runner. But . . . '

'Of course! Gwendoline left Whiteladies long before you started working here, didn't she? Now, what can I tell you about her tastes?' mused Mrs Paslew with a thoughtful frown. 'Well, she loves children and music, and she adored drawing wildflowers as a girl. Indeed, that's how she met her husband. Simon is a botanist. Gwendoline is a keen gardener, too. It was she who planted and tended the herb garden at Whiteladies — she never allowed Dobson or the garden boys anywhere near it while she was living here. I'm afraid I can't think of anything else useful, Amy.'

'I'm sure that'll be enough, ma'am.' Amy nodded, in her mind's eye seeing how pretty a delicate pattern of herbs and wildflowers might look upon a baby's shawl and nightgowns and suchlike. 'I have some ideas already.'

'Splendid! You must make a list of the materials you'll need and purchase everything while you're in Liverpool. I'll have a word with Mrs Braithwaite, too. Although you'll continue to help her, you'll need plenty of time away from the kitchen to devote to your needlework. You may go now, Amy.' Eleanor Paslew smiled, picking up her letter once more. 'We'll have another talk before you depart for Liverpool.'

★   ★   ★

Impatient to share her news with Dan, the instant Amy spotted him coming towards the school-house to meet her she flew down the lane and flung herself into his arms. 'Dan — I'm to go to Liverpool with the Paslew sisters! We're to stay at a hotel and go shopping in Bold Street! But best of all, Mrs Paslew has asked me to embroider a layette for her first grandchild! I'm doing a pattern of wildflowers and herbs.' Becoming aware of the rigid set of his jaw, she stepped back from him. 'Whatever is it, Dan? I was delighted to be asked to do this!'

'Aye, I can see that plain as day,' he answered grimly. 'It's bad enough you spend every hour God sends skivvying for the Paslews, without them piling on extra work and sending you away from your home to run their errands for them!'

'I enjoy sewing, and it'll be lovely making the baby things,' replied Amy, slipping her arm through his as they walked with Vicky hopscotching on ahead. 'I'm glad Mrs Paslew and Miss Clemmie think I'm a good needlewoman. It's nice having my work appreciated.'

'From where I stand, they're taking

advantage, plain and simple.'

'Don't be churlish, Dan!' she rebuked mildly. 'I thought you'd be pleased for me!'

'I'll not be pleased until the day you leave Whiteladies Grange! I can't stomach the notion of you waiting on the Paslews hand and foot.'

'Well, I'm thrilled about all this! Mrs Paslew said I'm to spend less time in the kitchen to make more time for sewing — and I'd far rather sew than scour pots and pans for Gladys Braithwaite!' She hugged his arm, determined not to let her happy mood be dampened. 'I was a bit apprehensive about going to Liverpool, but now I'm looking forward to it. Aunt Anne will keep an eye on things at Clockmakers Cottage, and I have to set off really early on Thursday morning because the coach comes — '

'I do know when the Liverpool coach comes through.' He expelled a disconcerted breath. 'Liverpool's a long way off, Amy. You've not the slightest notion what you might be letting yourself in for.'

'I'm accompanying Miss Sophie and Miss Clemmie and doing some errands for Mrs Paslew,' she explained patiently. 'I'm also to buy whatever I need for the layette from Mosley's in Bold Street — that's the haberdasher's where Mr Gilbert bought my silver scissors. Although Aunt Anne's never been to Liverpool, she's heard of Mosley's and says it's the finest haberdashery in the whole of Lancashire. This isn't like you at all, Dan,' she said softly, reaching up to brush his rough cheek with a kiss. 'Why can't you be happy for me?'

'I can't be happy you're going away, Amy, even for a day.' He frowned, tightening his grip upon her hand. 'I don't want you gallivanting all over the show with the likes of them. I want you here — with me!'

'Dan!'

Their tender kiss was interrupted by Vicky's shouting for them to hurry and catch up, because she couldn't clamber over the stile on her own.

'What's *he* doing at Clockmakers?'

exclaimed Dan, in the distance spotting Gilbert Paslew leaving the cottage and cantering towards the bridle path running through Friars Wood.

'Who? Oh, Mr Gilbert. He'll have been helping Teddy with his studies. Aunt Anne says he's a first-rate scholar.' She bundled Vicky over the high, jagged stones of the sea-facing stile. 'Will you stay for supper tonight? I've made plum cobbler for afters.'

'Can't refuse that, can I?' He grinned, adding seriously, 'I wish you wouldn't go to Liverpool, Amy. It's a place like you can never even imagine until you've actually seen it with your own eyes. When I was about Edmund's age I went a couple of times in Collie Barraclough's hay-cart. It's a huge, filthy, dark place. There's smoke and dirt and noise, and people crammed together on the streets so close you could scarce put a pin between them.' He shook his head in disgust. 'And the air's so foul, you're loath to breathe it in.'

'That's not how Pa speaks of the town, and he sails there with the *Jenet Rae* often,' remarked Amy. 'Aren't there fine buildings and grand shops and hotels and magnificent ships that sail around the whole world?'

'Aye, there's that and more. The town's got brass, no doubt about that,' he admitted soberly. 'But next to the big houses and fancy carriages and concert halls, there's folk in rags and beggars on every corner. You must be on your guard every minute. The streets are teeming with vagabonds and cut-throats who prey on strangers.' Dan touched a hand to her cheek, meeting her gaze with troubled eyes. 'I mean it, Amy. You take care — great care! Liverpool's a dangerous place for a young lass alone.'

6

Upon her arrival in Liverpool, Amy found Dan's vivid description of the thriving port coming to life all around her. Accustomed to Monks Quay, where open sea, meadow and woodland stretched as far as the eye could see, and even in the town most faces were familiar, here Amy's senses were assaulted. She felt swallowed up by walls and crowds pressing in all about her. Soot-blackened buildings towered high above the carriage as it crawled to the hotel along a maze of dark cobbled streets crammed with vehicles of every kind and seething with jostling, hurrying people of colours and costumes she'd never seen before, speaking in tongues and dialects foreign and rapid to her ears. Everywhere was noise, bustle and thick, choking chimney smoke.

At Clemmie's behest, Amy accompanied the sisters to the milliner, but declined the opportunity to go with them to their dressmaker. Mindful of the list of errands she needed to complete for Mrs Paslew, she was anxious to be off and started. She'd thought it gallant when Gilbert Paslew offered to escort her on her errands, however Amy was aware he was in Liverpool to conduct business for his father, and besides, she was keen to prove herself capable of finding her own way and managing without help. She was also hoping to slip away down to the river and see all the magnificent ocean-going brigs and schooners and clippers and barques Pa spun thrilling yarns about. How surprised and pleased he'd be when he next brought the *Jenet Rae* home to Monks Quay and Amy told him she'd been on a trip of her own!

As soon as Mrs Paslew's errands were done, the fabrics, silks, buttons and ribbons for the layette chosen and purchased, and arrangements made for the parcels and boxes to be promptly delivered to the hotel, she sought directions to the docks. Acutely aware of Dan's warnings and the crush of people and traffic surging along the streets, she walked briskly through the town and in but minutes glimpsed topsails in the near distance. Turning a sharp corner, the dull swell of murky waves lay before her, and she gasped to see scores of vessels — three, four, five abreast — at anchor and the swarms of men, women, children, pack-horses, carts and barrows milling like colonies of busy insects all along the waterfront.

She stood, drinking in each sight and sound so she might relate every last detail to Teddy and Vicky, Aunt Anne and Pa. She was taking a final look at it all when she saw Rory walking straight past her, not more than a few yards away. For a split second, she just stared. He was already being absorbed by the crowd.

'Rory!' Amy went after him, but he did not turn around and she had to break into a run, grabbing at his arm when at last he was within her reach. 'Rory!'

'How did you find me?' He glared sharply at her, his shrewd eyes sliding beyond his sister to scan the mass of faces moving around them. 'Who's with you?'

'Nobody! Rory, you disappeared without a word — are you all right? What are you doing here?'

'Working,' he spat. 'What does it look like I'm doing?'

'Are you working for Theodore Buxton still?' she asked quietly, noting his appearance for the first time. Although not as smartly dressed as Fanny had described, he was cleanshaven, well-clad and had a certain air of authority in his bearing. 'Is that why you were in York recently? To see Theodore?'

'I don't know you, and you don't know me. Get it? Now be on your way.' He started from her without another glance. 'Do yourself a favour, Amy — don't look back!'

Despite the warmth of the day, a chill of foreboding shuddered down the length of Amy's spine. Unsure what to do next, she followed him at a distance, watching him shoulder his way through the crowds.

He presently veered toward a massive red-bricked, sea-facing building six storeys high, with row upon row of small windows along the uppermost floors. There he paused, spoke briefly to an older man dressed in working clothes who was loading a wagon with kegs, and vanished within the dark confines of the cavernous building.

Amy slowly retraced her steps. What on earth was Rory doing in Liverpool? It was a long way from Monks Quay. And from York! If he and Theodore were still in league — and somehow Amy was certain Rory *was* still working for Fanny's husband — in what nefarious activity were the pair engaged? And how was Rory connected to that vast building on the waterfront?

An old seaman who'd lost a leg and been forced to eke out a living ashore was selling newspapers outside a chandlery. He probably knew everyone and everything that passed him by. Amy stopped, politely enquiring about the building Rory had entered.

'Customs ware'ouse, miss.' The sailor tapped snuff onto the back of his hand and inhaled. 'Full to the rafters with ships' cargo. Can't come out till the duty gets paid on it, see?'

Amy didn't, but she would ask Dan about that when she went home to Monks Quay. 'What sorts of cargo is kept in there?'

'Want to know a lot, don't 'ee?' He squinted up at her suspiciously. 'Fancy stuff, that's what. Brandy, rum, tea, spices and all such else. Now do you want to buy the paper or no'?'

Clutching a newspaper and suddenly aware of the lateness of the afternoon, Amy sped from the river, up through the town to the hotel. She'd been far longer than intended and was worried lest the Paslew sisters had returned and were angrily waiting for her to attend them. But she need not have been concerned, for when she hurried flushed and breathless into the hotel lobby, Gilbert Paslew rose from one of the sofas and immediately set her mind at ease.

'No sign of my sisters yet.' He smiled, offering Amy his arm. 'Looks as though we'll have to go to tea without them.'

'I can't do that!' she cried without thinking, catching her breath and straightening her bonnet. 'I'll have to see to them when they get back.'

'It would be an act of compassion, Miss Macfarlene,' he went on, firmly propelling her towards the brass and mahogany revolving doors. 'After a day spent negotiating contracts with various quite unscrupulous individuals, I'm sorely in need of civilised companion-ship, together with a pot of fine tea and a substantial plate of madeleines. Rather than here at the hotel, I recommend we take tea at a very pleasant tea shop not far from the library,' he said, sweeping her out into the late-afternoon sunshine. 'Then perhaps a stroll through the gar-dens? There's often a band that plays at that hour, too. You do like music, don't you?'

'This is ridiculous, Mr Gilbert!' Amy said, aware of his hand resting lightly upon her arm and keeping her at his side. 'I can't just go off. What about Miss Clemmie and Miss Sophie?'

Gilbert shrugged and smiled down at her, his grey eyes alight. 'Let them get their own tea and madeleines.'

It was a lovely afternoon. Tea. The band playing wonderful tunes. Walking with Gilbert through the gardens. Every moment was perfect! Amy hadn't given a thought to her encounter with Rory, nor even to repercussions with the Misses Paslew, until they were entering the hotel once more. The carefree happiness of the afternoon seemed to melt away into the dusk, and Amy couldn't quite believe she'd spent the past hours alone with Gilbert Paslew. Suddenly feeling very much the servant again, she was anxious to return where she belonged and moved from his side, lowering her eyes.

'It — it was really nice,' she murmured awkwardly. 'Thank you.'

'The thanks are all mine, Miss Macfarlene. I can't recall when I've enjoyed an afternoon more.' Touching a hand to

Amy's elbow, Gilbert accompanied her to the sweeping staircase. 'I suppose I'd better look in on my sisters. By the way, you will join us for dinner this evening, won't you?'

'No!' she exclaimed in horror, adding quietly, 'That is, it wouldn't be appropriate, sir.'

'We aren't in the autocratic realm of Whiteladies Grange and Monks Quay now!' he declared dismissively. 'You'll have to eat anyway, won't you? Very well, then. I'll call for you at eight and we'll all go down together.'

The prospect of dining with the Paslews in a grand hotel was not one Amy looked forward to. Even wearing her best dress, she felt homely and horribly out of place until Clemmie slipped her arm through hers, and the two girls descended the staircase together, entering the dining-room chatting and smiling about the day's excursions.

It was a fine meal with much lively conversation and laughter. After relating a humorous incident at the glover's, the irrepressible Sophie launched into her intentions for captivating Laurence Deane when he and Amelia came to stay at Whiteladies Grange later that month. 'And Gilbert,' she said blithely, 'I shall be relying upon *you* to entertain Amelia!'

'Not again! Besides — ' He glanced sidelong and winked at Amy. ' — I'll be bookkeeping for Father's brick kilns that day.'

'Which day?' challenged Sophie.

'Whichever day you want me to entertain Amelia Deane.'

'If you don't help me woo Laurence, I'll become an old maid,' Sophie said threateningly. 'Because brothers are duty-bound to provide for their spinster sisters, you'll have me living with you for the rest of your life!'

'Good Lord, anything but that!' Gilbert grimaced, catching Amy's eye again. 'What choice does a man have, but to do precisely as his sister bids?'

'That's settled then.' Lowering her voice, Sophie looked around the table conspiratorially. 'I have a wooing plan, and it's absolutely foolproof.'

It was very late when Amy climbed into bed in the bare little room at the end of the rear corridor set aside for the hotel guests' maids, boot boys and valets. It had been quite a day and she slept almost at once, her last waking thought of seeing Dan again on the morrow.

★ ★ ★

'Well done, everyone! That was a fine effort, especially from the trebles!' Reverend William Linley said after All Hallows' weekly choir practice. The elderly man leaned heavily on his cane, glancing benignly to the fidgeting little boys on the front row who were longingly eyeing the sunshine beyond the open west door. 'Before you rush away and into mischief, I have a short announcement. You'll be relieved to know that instead of having to put up with me muddling my way through the sheet music, you're to have a proper choirmaster once more! I've twisted my nephew's arm, and he's agreed to step into the breach. Gilbert?'

Along with the rest of the choir, Amy watched Gilbert Paslew make his way from the rear of the stalls down to Reverend Linley's side. 'I'm proud to have been asked to become choirmaster, and I'll do my very best to be a good one.' Gilbert smiled across at the singers, his quiet voice resonating around the centuries-old church. 'Of course, I'll still be singing with you, and playing the organ whenever it's my turn to do so. And although harvest festival is still a while off, I'm already planning the music for our service of thanksgiving. If any of you have any suggestions for hymns or music, do let me know. It'd be nice to have some fresh ideas. A final point, as harvest approaches, please remember to give as much as you're able for those less fortunate than ourselves, whether it be food, fuel, warm clothing or other comforts. Needless to say, we'll also need lots of pairs of hands to deliver baskets to the needy of our parish after harvest festival is over. We'll begin rehearsals for the service next week,' he said, his tanned face breaking into a warm smile. 'Meanwhile, I'll see you all bright and early on Sunday morning!'

The choir dispersed and began leaving the church. Gilbert and Reverend Linley were talking quietly beside the pulpit and as Amy went by, the vicar called out to her. 'Amy! Can you spare a few minutes?' he asked hopefully. 'Will you come across to the rectory? Mrs Linley — well, both of us, really — would like to ask you something.' He started toward the vestry, his steps slow and awkward despite the cane, and Amy followed.

'Sounds important,' Gilbert said with a smile as she passed him. 'Good luck!'

★   ★   ★

'The vicar and Mrs Linley have asked me to start a Sunday school, Dan!' Amy told him while they were apple-picking in the little mixed orchard beyond Clockmakers Cottage. 'When we were young, Mrs Linley took Sunday school. After she became poorly, it stopped.'

'I wouldn't know,' he commented from the top of the ladder. 'I never went.'

'I remember!' she said. 'Fancy them asking *me* to run a Sunday school!'

'You said you'd do it, didn't you?'

'Of course I did! Sunday school is very important. It's a lovely way for the little ones to learn. I'm beginning next Sunday.'

'It's nice you were asked and all,' he conceded. 'But Sunday is the only time you get a few hours away from White-ladies Grange. Now you won't even have that, because you'll be at the church all day long. It's yet another chore you've got to go and do.'

'I *want* to take the Sunday school, Dan!' she cried in surprise, craning her neck to look up at him. 'It isn't a chore!'

'What about you and me, Amy?' he responded, unhooking the apple-bag from across his chest. 'When is there going to be time for us to be together?'

'We see each other lots of the time!'

168

Taking the weight of the bag, she laid it onto the grass and knelt to begin sorting the fruit. 'And we spend nice days like this together.'

'We *see* each other, aye, but . . . ' Dan's gaze drifted the length of the orchard with its mature trees bearing plums, damsons and pears as well as apples, where Amy's brother and sister and Nicholas Buxton were also picking fruit, and plumped for simply changing the subject altogether. 'You decided to tell Edmund about meeting Rory in Liverpool, then? He mentioned it last night at the Mermaid.'

Amy nodded, arranging the apples carefully in the trug so they wouldn't bruise. 'I thought long and hard about it. In the end, I said only that I'd seen Rory and spoken to him. Nothing more. I don't want Teddy knowing anything about Rory's wrongdoing, but it's dreadful keeping things from him, Dan. It seems so underhand!'

'Maybe so,' he replied, climbing from the top rung up into the boughs. 'It'd do Edmund no good to know what we know, though, so why give him the burden of it?'

'That's true enough.' She straightened up, arching her aching back. 'I'm guilty and ashamed because I know it was Rory who attacked Sydney Wallace, and yet I've done nothing to bring about justice. I don't ever want Teddy feeling this shame.'

'You're not to blame, Amy. There's only one who is, and he won't be losing any sleep dwelling on it.'

'What do you suppose Rory and Theodore are up to in Liverpool?' she ventured soberly. 'Have you heard anything? News coming in with the coach, I mean?'

'I hear all sorts of talk and tales at the Mermaid, but nowt particular,' he answered. 'A man like Buxton has all the right connections. It'd be my guess he does the organising from a gentlemanly distance, while Rory's down in the thick of it. He's a hard man, your brother. There's not many who'd be willing to cross him.'

'Especially when he's carrying a pistol,' she murmured grimly. 'Rory told me he was working.'

'Thieving, more like,' Dan returned scornfully. 'The old sailor said it was a customs warehouse, didn't he? All sorts of valuable cargo is stored in them places, just there for the taking! Rory and Buxton are likely getting rich selling stolen goods to wealthy folk who'll happily turn a blind eye to avoid paying the government its duty.'

'Rory will go to gaol if he's caught, won't he?' Amy remarked bleakly. 'Or face transportation.'

'They're playing a dangerous game, gambling on being too clever to get caught,' replied Dan harshly. 'And who knows? Maybe Rory and Buxton are slippery enough to get away with it.' He shinned down the ladder, standing at her side and looking across the orchard to the damsons. 'Do you reckon he knows anything about his brother's shenanigans?'

'I doubt it very much. Nick's a decent sort,' responded Amy, following his gaze to where Nicholas Buxton was holding the ladder tightly while Vicky filled her basket with damsons from the low boughs. 'He's a kind man and he thinks about others, which is more than can be said for his older brother — or mine!'

Vicky scrambled down the ladder and ran over, her bonnet askew and the damson basket clutched in both arms. 'I've picked lots, Amy! Can we bake a pie now? Can we? And have it for tea?'

'Apple and damson pie would go down well, Amy,' chipped in Edmund from the heights of his pear tree.

'It'd be just the job after spending a whole day picking the brutes,' chimed in Dan. 'How about it, Amy?'

'On one condition,' she said, looking to Nicholas. 'Vicky and I will make a pie if Nick promises to stay and share it!'

'Rather!' exclaimed Nicholas, pleased. 'You're the best cook in the whole world, Amy — heaps better than Mrs Braithwaite at Whiteladies!'

'That's settled then.' Straightening

Vicky's bonnet, Amy picked up her trug of apples. 'Come on, Vicky — we've a pie to bake!'

Hand in hand, the sisters walked through the orchard towards Clockmakers Cottage, leaving the men to their fruit-picking.

⋆   ⋆   ⋆

It was a warm afternoon, and Amy had conducted her first Sunday school underneath the shady trees beside the north transept. She was clearing up when Gilbert Paslew came across from the rectory.

'May I help?' He stooped and started gathering up slates and books without waiting for an answer. 'How did it go?'

'Well, I think . . . ' She laughed, crossing her fingers. 'I hope!'

'From what I saw when Uncle William and I got back from parish visits, it was a great success,' he responded, following her into church. 'The children were utterly absorbed when you were reading to them.'

'The parable of the good shepherd.' She smiled, stacking the books into the cupboard. 'Aren't you here very early for the service?'

'I'm considering introducing a little of Mozart's sacred music into evensong. But since I haven't played it for a while, I decided practice would be a sensible idea,' he answered, leafing through the sheet music he'd brought with him. 'Amy, will you tell me what you think about my playing, and whether you believe this piece is suitable for evensong?'

'Gladly. If it's anything like the music you were playing when Reverend and Mrs Linley were at Whiteladies the other evening, I'm sure it will suit perfectly well.' She glanced up at him, her warm brown eyes dancing. 'Although you do realise some of the congregation will be up in arms because it's different?'

'Ah!' He nodded gravely. 'Accusations of heresy, you surmise?'

'At the very least.'

'Well, the worst that can happen is my being struck off the organ-playing rota and banished from Monks Quay,' he replied, adding, 'Which reminds me — Nicholas asked me to tell you he'll call at Clockmakers Cottage after supper tonight to say his goodbyes.'

Amy nodded. 'His coach leaves at first light tomorrow. Nick's really become part of the family. We're all going to miss him a lot, especially Vicky. She loves having another big brother to play games with.'

'Nicholas mentioned something about collecting a box, too. He said you'd understand?'

'I do. He's taking letters from us all, and a box of this summer's jams and bottled fruit, and some of Aunt Anne's cordial and honeys back to York with him for Fanny. I don't suppose Fanny does her own baking anymore, so I'm sending her a plum cake and an apple pie from Clockmakers' orchard as well.'

'You miss your sister a great deal, don't you?'

'Mmm. We write regularly, but it isn't the same as talking to her properly,' confided Amy with a smile.

'Why don't you take the coach and go with Nicholas to York tomorrow?' Gilbert exclaimed impulsively. 'You could visit your sister for a while.'

'Go to York?' she echoed, astonished. 'How could I do that?'

'I'm sure your aunt would look after Vicky,' he went on enthusiastically. 'And a leave of absence from Whiteladies Grange can easily be arranged.'

'No!' she cried, shaking her head. 'No, Gilbert. I couldn't!'

'All you need do is pack and board the coach,' he persisted amiably. 'I'll see to arranging your seat and everything.'

'You don't understand.' She frowned, unable to explain. 'It wouldn't — wouldn't be proper.'

'Amy, I'm sorry!' Gilbert exclaimed earnestly, reaching out and catching her fingers, and holding her still when she would have moved from him. 'I didn't mean to offend you.'

Involuntarily, Amy gasped. Her eyes were drawn to their joined hands.

Following her gaze, Gilbert gently released her.

'I believed we had become friends, Amy.' His grey eyes were solemn. 'I know you miss your sister, and would very much have liked to give the happiness of visiting her to you.'

*   *   *

The next morning, Amy decided to leave Clockmakers Cottage earlier than usual and see Nick off aboard the York-bound coach before going on to Whiteladies Grange. Gilbert Paslew had ridden into town with him, and the two men were already at the Mermaid when Amy arrived. It was chilly, and they ushered her inside to the warmth of the inn's blazing fire.

'I've never really had a family before, Amy,' said Nicholas shyly. 'My dear sister! I can't tell you what it's meant to be part of a real family these past months! I understand how you feel about Monks Quay — if it were my home, I'd never want to leave, either.'

'You'll always have a home here with us, Nick.' She swallowed hard. 'Come back soon!'

The horn blew. They went out once more into the damp, misty morning and saw the coach making ready to leave. Dan Ainsworth had harnessed fresh horses and was helping the driver load the last of the baggage.

Nicholas climbed aboard, settling into his seat. 'I'll be sure to give Fanny your box the moment I get to Carteret Square.'

'It's not too late to change your mind,' Gilbert murmured close to Amy's ear. 'Are you certain you don't want to go to York?'

Amy merely nodded, returning Nick's wave as the coach rattled away from the Mermaid Inn at a cracking pace.

'You don't have to be up at White-ladies for a bit yet,' Dan said, striding across the cobbles to her side. 'Come in for some chocolate. There's a real nip in the air today!'

'Autumn's not far off,' she replied,

glancing back at Gilbert. 'Are you coming in?'

'I don't think so.'

'I'm glad you weren't pilloried for the Mozart.'

'It's early days yet!' He grinned, gathering up the reins of both horses before mounting his bay. 'I'll see you at choir practice — all being well.'

The inn was unusually peaceful and quiet. It was still too early for the Mermaid's guests to be up and about, and the next coach wasn't due for another couple of hours. Dan and Amy sat companionably at the fireside, warmth and silence enveloping them as they sipped steaming cups of strong chocolate.

'It could always be like this for us, Amy,' Dan murmured, kissing her hair, 'if we were wed.'

'Dan?' She twisted around on the settle to face him.

'I mean it,' he responded simply. 'Let's get married.'

'Married? I-I've never even thought . . . Well, not really,' she stammered at length. 'Anyway, I can't get married, Dan. Not yet.'

'Because of the family? I know you've your da and Vicky and Edmund to think about, but that's no reason not to get married,' he went on practically. 'You can be my wife and still look after them. Your da's at sea most of the time, and Edmund'll be going away to school once he gets his scholarship. That just leaves Vicky, and we'll look after her together. She's a grand little lass.'

Amy sighed deeply. 'I can't marry you, Dan. It isn't because of the family — it's *me*,' she whispered, unable to meet his eyes. 'I care for you very much. You're my best friend in all the world, but . . . I'm so sorry,' she faltered miserably, finally raising her gaze to his. 'I'm just not sure enough of my feelings.'

'That's all right, lass. I'm sure of mine for you.' He drew her closer into his arms. 'And I shall go on asking until you're sure of yours and you say yes!'

* * *

Dan has asked me to marry him, wrote Amy a few days later. Clockmakers Cottage was uncomfortably hot, and she'd left Teddy studying with Gilbert Paslew in the sitting-room and taken her writing tablet into the garden. It was no cooler out there; not a breath of breeze was coming in from the sea. The sky was low and white and the air sultry.

> *You've often teased me about Dan, and how I should 'snap him up' the first chance I go, but I just couldn't accept. Yet I think I must love Dan, because I'm happy whenever we're together and I don't know what I'd do without him. Is it love, Fan?*
>
> *You were so sure about Theodore! But I just don't know if marrying Dan would be the right thing to do. Oh, if only I could see you and talk to you about all this!*
>
> *You'll never guess what happened the day before Nick left for York. Out of the blue, Gilbert Paslew said he'd get me a seat on the coach so I*

*could travel with Nick and visit you!
I was quite shocked at first, then I
was very tempted. Obviously, it was
out of the question. I realise Gilbert
meant it kindly and honourably, but
it would've been improper for me to
accept a favour of that sort, don't you
think? Can you imagine what Pa
would say when he came ashore and
found out? He'd be furious! Pa'd
think it the most awful insult to me,
and to the family.*

*You know how bitterly he feels about
the Paslews. Actually, Pa even disapproves of Gilbert helping Teddy with
his scholarship work. It isn't fair for
Pa to have a grudge against Gilbert
simply because he's Alfred Paslew's
son.*

Amy was sitting on the parched grass
beneath the apple tree, her head bowed
over the tablet resting upon her lap. The
afternoon grew hotter and even more
oppressive. By and by, perspiration
trickled down her forehead and neck,

and she'd already heard the distant rumble of thunder far out across the sea when Edmund and Gilbert emerged from Clockmakers Cottage. Teddy had been rather low in spirits of late, and Amy had wondered if his studies and the stable-work at the Mermaid were becoming too much for him. He looked much brighter now, however.

Setting aside her letter to finish later, Amy smiled up at him. 'How are you getting on?'

'Better! Not before time, either,' Edmund said with a grin, and added, 'I've been struggling with Latin for weeks and weeks, but at long last it is starting to make sense.'

'Well done, Teddy! All your efforts are bringing good results.'

'Anne was absolutely right about Edmund,' put in Gilbert, offering his hand to help Amy rise from the grass. 'Your brother does have outstanding ability, though that alone counts for little without the will to work hard and persevere even when the task seems impossible. The scholarship examination won't have a worthier candidate, nor one more deserving of the award.'

'I've still a long way to go before the examination,' commented Edmund sensibly, trying not to look too pleased. 'Are you both off to choir practice now?'

The pair nodded, bade Edmund goodbye, and presently started away across the meadows beyond clockmakers Cottage, their easy conversation soon turning to the harvest festival preparations.

'Now we've had a few rehearsals,' Amy was saying as they strolled through the tinderdry, knee-high grasses, 'the choir is starting to really get a feel for the music. And it's a nice change to have the youngest children singing a few hymns on their own.'

'Yes, they do seem to like doing that, don't they?' reflected Gilbert. 'It was hearing the little ones singing at your Sunday school that gave me the idea, actually. I thought it might help them feel more involved.'

A shuddering growl of thunder followed

by a sky-splitting crack of yellow lightning drowned his words. The heavens opened and the storm broke. Dragging off his coat, Gilbert wrapped it tightly about Amy's shoulders. Rain was coursing down his face. She knew he was shouting but couldn't hear a word. With an arm securely about Amy's waist, he pointed across the meadow, and with heads bowed into the driving rain they ran for Burlham's barn.

Soaked to the skin and breathless, they burst through the broken timber doors into the tumbledown barn. Apart from a few bales of old sorry-looking hay, a rusting plough and various other forgotten tools, the barn was empty and hadn't seen use or repair since old Miss Burlham's brother passed away. The broken roof leaked like a sieve, and they weren't much drier inside than they would have been out in the teeth of the thunderstorm.

'I suppose it's better than standing under a tree!' commented Gilbert, watching a brilliant fork of lightning snake across the leaden sky. 'If the whole place doesn't collapse around us, we should be fine.'

Amy laughed, but couldn't stop dithering. The temperature was plummeting and she was wet through, her sodden clothing clinging to her cold skin.

'You're shivering.' Gilbert pulled the coat tighter about her, taking her white hands into his own and rubbing them vigorously. 'Any better?'

'Much, thank you.'

Gilbert didn't release her. Murmuring her name, his grey eyes lingered upon her face and lips. 'Amy, I . . . '

Amy's heart was pounding so hard she couldn't breathe. She could only stand there, gazing up at him while the storm raged all around and the moments ticked away. A rapid explosion of lightning flashes illuminating the shadowy barn into flickering brilliance jolted Amy back to her senses. Even then, she had immense difficulty breaking the spell between them, and taking that single step away from him.

'I think the rain is stopping,' she got out at last, tearing her attention away from Gilbert to the world outside. 'We ought to go. We — we'll be late for choir practice.'

The drenched meadow was sparkling in the watery sunlight when they emerged from Burlham's barn and continued onwards to All Hallows. With Gilbert's coat still around her, Amy was trembling, her legs weak at the knees. From time to time, she cast a sideways glance at the man walking at her side. They hadn't spoken since leaving the barn, but somehow it was a perfectly companionable silence. When Gilbert held the west door for her to enter the church, she looked up at him, their eyes meeting for the first time.

Suddenly, Amy's pulse was racing and her senses suffused with new awareness. Dan Ainsworth had asked her to marry him. She couldn't imagine life without Dan, and yet . . . since those treacherous moments in Burlham's barn, Amy had been aching for Gilbert Paslew's kiss.

★ ★ ★

Amy had no notion of whether she remembered the words during choir practice, or even if she sang in tune. Such was her distraction, she could think only of Gilbert, and the surge of emotion he'd stirred within her. When she ordinarily would have paused to speak with him after practice ended, this evening she was relieved to see another member of the choir engaging him with some question or other. Slipping away unnoticed, she wondered if Gilbert felt as she did. If her longings had been laid bare for him to see when they'd stood at the church door and he'd looked down into her eyes . . .

The air had freshened somewhat since the storm, and stepping out into the cool twilight, Amy scurried down the path from All Hallows. She was too absorbed by her thoughts to notice the figure waiting within the lichgate, and started violently when Dan Ainsworth stepped out onto the path before her, his face angry and resentful.

'I saw you!' He caught her arm, hauling her into the confines of the ancient gate. 'I saw you with *him*!'

Amy's heart was thumping in her chest. 'What — whatever do you mean?'

'You know full well!' he retorted, his eyes boring into her. 'I planned to meet you on your way to choir, but I was held up at the Mermaid so I was late. Then I spotted the pair of you running into Burlham's barn — and saw *him*, with his hands on you!'

'You're making it sound — '

'Deny it, Amy! Deny it if you can!'

'It wasn't *like* that!' she cried vehemently. 'The storm started and Gilbert lent me his coat and we sheltered in the barn — that's all!'

'Then marry me, Amy,' mumbled Dan thickly, pulling her hard against him. 'I'm done with waiting, lass. Marry me *now*!'

7

Amy was hurrying along Abbotsgate and had just passed the Mermaid Inn when Edmund sprinted out from the archway and called after her. 'What are you doing in town?' he asked, catching her up.

'Collecting a book and some stationery Miss Clemmie ordered from Jessup's. Are you finished for the day?'

'Almost.' Edmund fell silent as Dan Ainsworth crossed Abbotsgate from the opposite side and strode towards them, watching Amy's changing expression.

'Hello, Dan,' she said quietly.

'Amy.' He nodded curtly, going past them into the Mermaid.

Edmund looked from Dan's rigid back to his sister's dismayed face. 'What's going on between you two? Have you fallen out?'

'It's complicated, Teddy.'

'Something's happened, hasn't it? I have to work with Dan every day, and he's like a bear with a sore head. He hasn't been to Clockmakers for ages, and he barely spoke to you just now.'

Amy hesitated, gazing past him into the distance, her eyes as bleak as the dull sky. 'Dan asked me to marry him.'

'And you said no?' he exclaimed incredulously. 'But you and Dan . . . I thought you were bound to get married!'

'I'll see you at home tonight.' She sighed dismally.

'Wait!' Pulling a letter from his coat, Edmund offered it to her. 'From Fanny. It came on this morning's coach. That's why I called after you in the first place. Oh, and Amy, I think you've made a dreadful mistake, refusing Dan's proposal.'

*   *   *

Amy usually relished going into Jessup's. It was a misshapen, cluttered little shop wedged between the apothecary and the dusty offices of Seward and Seward, where generations of Sewards had drawn up wills, deeds and contracts for the inhabitants of Monks Quay since the town was but a village. She paused at Jessup's window, admiring the neatly bound new novels and volumes of poetry displayed next to piles of worn second-hand books of all types, before going inside. While Mr Jessup wrapped Clemmie Paslew's book and stationery, Amy browsed shelves filled with paintbrushes, watercolours, charcoal sticks, pens, writing tablets, wafers, sealing wax and bottles of ink.

Outside once more, with Clemmie's parcel under her arm, Amy was wondering if there was enough time to take a cup of tea and read Fanny's letter before she had to be back at Whiteladies Grange. It was set to be another long day, for Miss Sophie's special guests had arrived earlier in the week. It seemed to Amy the entire household was on pins over this visit from Amelia and Laurence Deane, and she'd already been scolded several times by Gladys Braithwaite for spending too much time sewing and not enough working in the kitchen.

With Fanny's much-awaited letter in her hand, Amy crossed Abbotsgate and pushed open the curtained door of Betty Bower's tearoom. Going down the three uneven steps, she sat at one of the neat corner tables, and was about to open Fanny's letter when the bell over the door jingled. Amy glanced up to see Gilbert Paslew raising his hat and coming inside, bowing his head to avoid the low beams in the brightly lit little tearoom.

'May I join you? Oh, I beg your pardon,' he said as he noticed the unopened letter in Amy's hands. 'I'm disturbing you.'

'Not at all!' She smiled, her subdued mood lifting a little at the mere sight of him. 'I'll read it later. It's from Fanny.'

'That reminds me — I must write to Nicholas this week.' He sat down and ordered a pot of tea, oatcakes and white cheese. 'I'm hungry! I missed breakfast — well actually, I escaped it. One shouldn't be ungracious about house guests, but I really will be relieved when Amelia Deane and her brother go home.'

'Are they enjoying their visit?' asked Amy, pouring the tea.

'Absolutely! Laurence has had a serious talk with Father, so it appears Sophie's plan was indeed foolproof.' He smiled at her above the rim of his teacup. 'We had a very pleasant time in Liverpool, didn't we?'

'Oh, yes! For once, I'll have something interesting to tell Pa when he comes ashore.'

'When is he due home?'

'In another week or so, though at this time of year the weather and tides can be very unpredictable. If the *Jenet Rae* isn't able to make the crossing, she'll have to wait in Ireland until conditions improve enough to set sail.'

'I'm afraid I don't know much about the packet,' Gilbert remarked thoughtfully. 'It must on occasion be very worrying for you. Your father has a dangerous occupation.'

'It certainly can be. But Pa loves the sea. Without it and his boat, he'd be — ' She broke off, blushing a little. 'Like a fish out of water! The sea is Pa's whole life. Always has been.'

'I envy — admire — somebody who has a real conviction of what he's meant to do in life,' reflected Gilbert seriously. 'I rather think my father has it — he appears to thrive on conducting business. I've spent the whole of today ensconced with young Mr Seward, poring over all sorts of legal matters connected with Father's various business interests.' He grinned and offered Amy an oatcake, helping himself to another. 'Small wonder I'm in need of sustenance! Another pot of tea?'

She shook her head. 'I really need to get on.'

'Me too.' He grimaced. 'I'm riding over to the brick kilns. Amy, have you been into the stationer's lately?'

'Just.'

'Did you read the notice about the play?' he asked. 'Marlowe's Company of Players are coming to Monks Quay and putting on *She Stoops to Conquer*. Do you know it?'

'I haven't been to many plays. Is it a good one?'

'I think you'd enjoy it. It's a very witty play, but it says something serious at the same time,' he replied, adding tentatively, 'Would you like to go to see it, Amy? Go with me, I mean?'

'Oh, yes!' she responded without thinking. 'Very much!'

'Splendid!' His grey eyes lit with pleasure. 'I'm sure we'll have a fine evening!'

After Gilbert had taken his leave, Amy lingered a few minutes more in the tearoom and opened Fanny's letter. After reading only a paragraph or two, she gasped in delight.

I'm not certain, Amy, so please do not breathe a word to a living soul. However, I'm accustomed to such robust health I really cannot imagine any other cause.

When Nicholas returned from Monks Quay, I was in floods of tears! Opening your box of treats and reading letters from you all left me quite undone! This isn't like me at all, Amy, and I'm feeling very impatient with myself.

However, I was immensely relieved to see Nicholas home again. Theo is away on business so frequently now, and I miss him dreadfully. I now realise how hard it must've been for Ma, spending so much time parted from Pa while he was at sea. At least my husband is only away for a few days, and even then by barely a coach ride's distance.

Obviously, I haven't spoken to Theo yet about my condition, but how his absences distress me! I confess to great loneliness in this fine big house, and wish with all my heart to be again part of the homely bustle in Clockmakers Cottage. I never imagined I would ever say that!

Perhaps, dear Amy, you had it right all along.

* * *

Amy's joy at the prospect of Fanny expecting a child was tempered by concern for her sister's well-being. The impulsive notion of travelling to York gradually strengthened with the passing days into firm resolve.

'I won't go until Pa comes ashore,' she told Edmund. 'I'll have to beg a leave of absence from Whiteladies, of course, but I don't think Mrs Paslew will refuse me.'

'Is Fanny ill?' Edmund's deepening voice registered alarm. 'You would tell me? I'm not a child!'

Amy hesitated. Although mindful of Fanny's request, she needed to reassure her young brother. 'Fanny might be expecting, and she isn't feeling very well. It's natural and nothing to be concerned about, but I think she needs me, Teddy. I'd really like to see her, too.'

'Can we afford it?'

'It'll mean emptying the caddy.'

'Is there enough in there?' Edmund glanced at Ma's old tea caddy, where the family saved whatever money they could spare. 'I bet the coach won't be cheap.'

'It isn't. I asked Mr Ainsworth.'

'Not Dan?' queried Edmund with a frown.

'Not Dan,' she replied flatly, meeting the reprove in Edmund's eyes. 'I now know for certain I could never marry him, but Dan still means so very much to me, Teddy. I wish there wasn't this awful coldness between us. I'd thought — hoped — we could've — '

'Gone on like before?'

'Remained friends.'

'I see Dan every day, Amy. I see how angry and hurt he is,' commented Edmund quietly. 'You really can't expect him to pretend he doesn't love you, or simply forget that you don't want to marry him.'

★   ★   ★

Although the poor weather delayed Ramsay Macfarlene bringing the *Jenet Rae* into Monks Quay by only four days, Amy was greatly relieved to hear the packet had tied up and Pa and his four crewmen were safely ashore. For no reason she could pin down, she'd felt a real foreboding about this particular trip, and was glad it was finally over and done without mishap to man nor boat.

'According to Ned Yarkin, Alfred Paslew and old Mr Seward had had their dinner at the Mermaid and were still there when word came that the *Jenet Rae* was coming in to harbour,' said Edmund, who'd run from the Inn to Whiteladies Grange with the news Pa was home. 'Anyhow, Mr Paslew went down to the quayside and met the packet. He and Pa came up to the Mermaid together. They're still there now.'

'How odd!' said Amy. It wasn't like Alfred Paslew to show any interest in the *Jenet Rae* at all, much less meet her at the quay. 'Were they just talking? Perhaps something is wrong. Did Mr Paslew seem annoyed?'

'No, they were all serious. Old Mr Seward was with them by then,' said Edmund thoughtfully. 'It just looked like they were having an important conversation together.'

'I don't know what to make of it.' Amy replied with a shake of her head. 'Thank you for coming to tell me Pa's back. What with the bad weather and everything . . . '

'I know. It was Dan who suggested I come and give you the news, Amy. He still really cares about you.'

'And I for him, but not in the way he wishes me to,' she murmured sadly. 'I expect I'll be late tonight, Teddy. The Paslews are having another dinner party.'

★ ★ ★

It *was* late when Amy arrived home to Clockmakers Cottage, and she was surprised to find Pa and Teddy, and Aunt Anne too, all waiting up for her.

'I wanted to wait until the whole family was together,' Ramsay said as soon as Amy was sitting down to her hotpot supper and bap. 'I've something to say.'

'A consequence of your meeting with Alfred Paslew at the Mermaid Inn?' enquired Anne matter-of-factly. 'What of it, Ramsay?'

'Paslew reckons he's neither the time nor the inclination to keep the packet going. He wants shot of the *Jenet Rae*.'

Amy was first to respond. 'What about you, Pa? Your job as skipper? And the crew?'

'Will the new owner keep you all on?' chipped in Edmund. 'Or will he be bringing in his own master and crew?'

Ramsay raised a hand. 'Steady now, we're getting ahead of ourselves here! There's no new owner. Not yet, at any rate.'

'Out with it, Ramsay,' said Anne a mite suspiciously. 'Tell us the worst!'

He drew in a measured breath before speaking. 'Paslew's offered me first refusal on the *Jenet Rae*. I've said I'll think on it.'

'He's done *what*?' demanded Anne in disbelief. 'The sheer gall of the man! You've been complaining for months the boat is scarcely seaworthy, and now Alfred Paslew is generously letting you take a pig in a poke off his hands — providing you pay good money for the privilege! Small wonder he's the richest man in Monks Quay.' She fixed her brother-in-law with a keen gaze. 'You're not seriously considering it, Ramsay? It's utter foolishness!'

'Begging your pardon, Anne, but I disagree,' he replied quietly. 'The *Jenet Rae* isn't as shipshape as she might be; I make no bones about that. But she's a well-built vessel, and stout at heart. There's nought wrong with her that can't be put right.'

'At what cost?' challenged Anne. 'I notice Alfred Paslew hasn't spent a farthing more than necessary on her.'

'That's true,' admitted Ramsay. 'Nor, in my opinion, did he ever have any proper interest in running the packet. Paslew has so many irons in the fire making huge profits for him, he's no time for the *Jenet Rae*. Happen she's more trouble than she's worth to him. But to *me* . . . '

'What, Pa?' prompted Amy gently, glimpsing a wistfulness in her father's expression. 'You want to buy her, don't you?'

'Aye, lass. Aye, I do,' he almost whispered, not meeting anyone's eyes. 'My whole life, I've doffed my hat and taken orders from whoever pays my wages — and been glad to do it. For that's what the likes of me does. But I've looked at them as does different and better, and I've envied them for it. Now, for the first time, I have the opportunity to be my own boss and make a secure future for my family.' Ramsay raised his eyes and met Anne's steadily. 'I don't want to let this chance pass me by, for at my time of life I'll surely never get another.'

'As owner, you would bear the entire responsibility of repairing, maintaining and sailing the vessel, as well as paying the crew and supporting your own family!' returned Anne curtly. 'From all I hear, the packet is hardly a thriving concern with Alfred Paslew behind it — why do you believe you can prosper where he does not?'

'Because I care about the *Jenet Rae*, and I *need* to make her prosper! What'll become of me when I'm too old to sail, if I don't have anything put by?' he went on earnestly. 'I've little enough learning, but I know the sea. I understand the weather and tides and cargos in ways Paslew has no inkling of. Over the years I've seen how the packet could be run better, and told Paslew so, but he took no heed. I know I can make a go of this, Anne. All I'm asking is for the chance to do it.'

The two stared at each other across the table, the only sound the shifting of glowing coals in the kitchen hearth.

Amy glanced from her aunt's grimly set face to Pa's anxious one. She didn't understand why he was so desperately seeking Aunt Anne's approval.

'I'm sorry, Ramsay. The risks are too great,' said Anne at last. 'As you are aware, I intend leaving the few material goods in my possession to Amy. I cannot — *will* not — risk losing everything by supporting this whim of yours. For should this foolhardy scheme fail, every last stick and farthing would indeed be lost!'

Anne Shawcross bid them goodnight, sweeping from Clockmakers Cottage into the night. After the door closed behind her, only the roar of the incoming tide and the groan of the offshore wind through the apple tree filled the shadowy kitchen.

'That's that, then.' Ramsay expelled a slow breath, rubbing the palms of his calloused hands over his face. 'In all fairness, I can't say I blame your aunt for deciding as she has. It must seem a crackpot scheme for the likes of me to run my own boat.'

'It doesn't!' exclaimed Amy, glancing quickly to Edmund, who nodded immediately. 'Teddy and I think you should buy the packet!'

'We believe in you, Pa!' Edmund enthused.

'Thanks, Ted. Thanks to both of you. I can't do it, though,' Ramsay answered simply. 'I've no money. The only way would've been to put up the cottage.'

'Sell Clockmakers?' cried Amy, adding at once, 'Well, if that's the only way to raise enough money, that's what must be done!'

'Nay, it wouldn't be sold,' explained Ramsay. 'Old Mr Seward was there when I was talking to Paslew, and he said if I put up Clockmakers Cottage as security, I could borrow enough money to buy the packet. It seemed a fair arrangement to me, and I told him so.' He glanced at his son and daughter. 'Thing is, Clockmakers isn't mine to do what I like with.'

'Not yours?' Amy said incredulously. 'But — '

'It's straightforward enough, lass. I've hardly ever had a spare guinea to my name, nor owned anything either. Your ma and Aunt Anne inherited Clock-makers Cottage from their parents, who'd already passed away when I met and married your ma. After a while, Anne moved into the schoolhouse so we could have the cottage to ourselves, but she still owns half of it.' He rose stiffly. 'I'm off to bed. Don't stay up too late, the pair of you.'

Brother and sister remained seated at the table. 'It explains a lot,' commented Edmund at length. 'I mean, we've never had much money, have we? Yet Clock-makers is a very nice cottage. With the garden and orchard and things.'

'I just took our home for granted, I suppose,' Amy said. 'Poor Pa! What can we do, Teddy?'

'You could try talking to Aunt Anne,' he suggested awkwardly. 'After all, she did say she was leaving everything to you. If it's going to be yours one day anyway — '

'Teddy, honestly!'

'I know, it's awful! I'm sorry. I couldn't think of anything else, that's all,' he admitted, shamefaced. 'Perhaps when Aunt Anne's thought it over, she'll change her mind.'

'Aunt Anne loves this cottage, Teddy. Clockmakers is her true home. I can well understand her being afraid of it being lost from the family. But if the packet's new owner doesn't keep Pa on as master, what will he do? He's not a young man anymore, and the sea is all he's ever known.'

* * *

Ramsay flatly refused to talk further about buying the *Jenet Rae*. Aunt Anne went to and from Clockmakers Cottage as usual, and Amy spent every available hour sewing. She was determined to complete the layette before she took her leave of absence from Whiteladies Grange and went to York.

Although the daily household routine

at Whiteladies was less hectic since Amelia and Laurence Deane's departure, the atmosphere was unusually lively and gay. Miss Sophie smiled and floated about the house on clouds, anticipating the formal announcement of her engagement; and for her part, Amy was constantly aware of Gilbert's presence. She caught herself hoping for a glimpse of him, listening for the deep tenor of his quiet voice, and occasionally felt the flutter of butterflies in her stomach if he entered the room where she was working.

Choir practice and Sundays at All Hallows became the happiest parts of the week, and it pleased Amy that Gilbert frequently sought her opinions and ideas upon his plans for the harvest festival. She was eagerly looking forward to going to the play with him, and when the day finally arrived, she wished Fanny was there to help her decide what to wear and how to arrange her hair becomingly.

'My word, you're looking a right

bobby dazzler!' exclaimed Ramsay when Amy came downstairs that evening. She was wearing her deep-green skirt and bodice, with the new lace collar and cuffs Fanny had made for her last birthday. 'Where are you off to?'

'There's a play on at the assembly rooms.' she explained, her cheeks pink. 'Gilbert's taking me to see it. He says — '

'Gilbert Paslew?' cut in Ramsay, his jaw set. 'You're not stepping out with Paslew's son this night or any other!'

'But he'll be here for me any minute!'

'He'll have a wasted journey then, won't he?' retorted Ramsay. 'I'll see him when he comes, and I want your word you'll not be meeting him again. At church and at Whiteladies Grange can't be helped, but otherwise you're to stay away from him, d'you hear?'

Amy stood silent, her spine rigid.

'Well? I'm waiting for your promise!'

Amy bit her lip. 'I can't promise, Pa. Gilbert and I are friends. He's invited me to the play, and I'm not letting him down.'

'What about letting yourself down? And your family?' he demanded angrily. 'What are you thinking of, Amy, going about with Paslew's son? I thought you'd have more sense!'

'That he's Alfred Paslew's son has nothing to do with it, Pa! I can't understand why you dislike him so! If only you knew him — '

'It's for your own good,' snapped Ramsay. 'You'll end up getting hurt if this goes on, my girl. There's a line in life, and if you know what's good for you, you don't step over it! Them as does come a cropper soon enough.'

'It's not fair!'

'Happen not, but the truth is the likes of them and the likes of us oughtn't mix, lass,' he said, a mite more gently. 'The sooner you face up to it, the better. Now be a good girl — go up and wait in your room until he's been and gone.'

She shook her head miserably. 'I can't do as you ask.'

'I'm not asking,' said Ramsay, his

temper sorely tested. 'I expect you to obey what — '

Amy heard the approaching carriage and, turning to the window, saw Gilbert drawing up alongside Clockmakers. 'I'm sorry, Pa.' Sweeping her cloak about her shoulders, Amy spun on her heel and was gone from the cottage to meet Gilbert Paslew at the gate.

'You look lovely!' Gilbert said with a smile, taking Amy's arm and helping her up into the seat. 'I'm so pleased you came.'

Amy had never seen a proper play performed before, and was delighted by the spectacle. The rooms and staircases of a medieval manor house appeared like magic upon the boards of the assembly rooms, and exquisitely costumed characters moved about this imaginary world, scheming and plotting and weaving a tale that held Amy spellbound until the makeshift curtain fell and she and Gilbert were filing out into the cool night air.

'It was wonderful!' exclaimed Amy happily. 'Every moment of it!'

During the drive from town, they discussed the play in detail, their conversation moving on to harvest festival, Sophie's forthcoming marriage, and somehow to Amy embroidering the layette.

'It's incredibly beautiful, Amy! I was there when Mother showed it to Clemmie and Sophie,' Gilbert was saying as the cobbles became sandy track and the carriage wheels and horse's hoofs were muffled. 'Herbs and wildflowers were such a clever choice for the design, too. Gwendoline will adore it! I'm really looking forward to being an uncle, although Gwen tells me I'm not to spoil my niece or nephew too much!'

'I might have a niece or nephew soon myself,' Amy said with a smile. 'I'll doubtless find out when I visit Fanny.'

'I wish you'd let me — '

'No, Gilbert,' she interrupted softly. 'Thank you, but no.'

He shrugged in resignation. 'When are you travelling to York?'

'I'm not sure. Things are a bit unsettled at home just now. Your father's offered to sell mine the *Jenet Rae*.'

'I didn't know. I wasn't even aware Father intended selling the packet. Is Mr Macfarlene going to buy it?'

'It's . . . complicated. Pa's to give his answer by the month's end, so I'll probably go to York after that and come home just before he sails on his next trip.'

They fell quiet for a while. It was a still, clear night with a scattering of stars, the rising moon but a silvery sliver. Tawny owls were flying, their calls and replies resonating from deep within the blackness of Friars Wood. The placid horse walked noiselessly onwards down the sandy, winding lane until the shore came into sight. The tide was far out, the pale, smooth sand stretching endlessly before them and gradually disappearing into the darkness.

'I'll miss you when you go away, Amy,' murmured Gilbert despondently. 'I don't suppose you have any use for a helpful and willing guide? I spent my boyhood at school in York, so I know all

215

the places of historic and cultural interest.'

Amy shook her head, her soft brown eyes laughing up at him.

'Thought not,' he said, suddenly catching his breath. Allowing the reins to fall from his fingers, he tenderly gathered Amy into his arms, his kiss deepening at the intensity of her response. Breathless and dizzy when their kiss finally ended, Amy nestled contentedly against him as he held her close and the horse plodded dutifully homewards.

All too quickly, the lights of Clockmakers Cottage slid into view and Amy was home. Apprehensive of the reception awaiting her, she was determined Gilbert should not sense her unease.

'I'll see you tomorrow!' he whispered, and their final parting kiss was as chaste as their first had been passionate.

A great many possibilities were coursing through Amy's mind when she pushed open the door and entered Clockmakers. However, she was quite unprepared to find Pa and Aunt Anne sitting together at the fireside. Immediately she saw her father's angry frown, but even as he was drawing breath, Aunt Anne was greeting her.

'Did you enjoy the play?' she asked with a smile, helping her niece off with her cloak. 'Gilbert mentioned you were both going to see it. He has such a fine appreciation of literature. I came here this evening to speak to your father,' Anne went on, fastening her bonnet. 'And I stayed to see you because I wanted to tell you myself — I've agreed to Clockmakers Cottage standing for your father's loan.' She raised a gloved hand, silencing Amy's exclamation. 'No, dear — there's nothing more to be said. It's done.'

*   *   *

Hours later, Amy was curled up on the oak chest gazing out from the window when Teddy appeared in the open doorway. 'May I come in?'

Tiptoeing past Vicky, who was

sleeping soundly with her rag doll, he sat beside Amy on the chest. 'What do you make of it all?'

'I'm surprised,' she admitted, her chin cupped in her hand. Truth to tell, she'd scarcely thought about the packet. Since coming upstairs, her thoughts had been of Gilbert. 'When I last spoke to Aunt Anne about Pa buying the boat, she still seemed set against it.'

'Well, whatever you said to her then must've done the trick!' He paused, following her gaze from the window to the lampblack sky. 'If the packet doesn't make enough money and we lose Clockmakers Cottage, what'll we do?'

'We'll manage, Teddy,' she replied with an optimism she scarcely felt. 'We'll manage, because we must.'

8

'We'll be ready to sail, all right!' Ramsay Macfarlene was saying enthusiastically when Amy and Vicky took his dinner to him aboard the *Jenet Rae*. 'We're not about to be late — not on our first trip!'

Amy nodded. The decks, hold and masts of the vessel were a hive of noise and activity as the crew and a handful of local men were striving to make good whatever repairs money and time allowed. The damp air was pungent with bubbling tar pots, wet hemp, fresh-sawn timbers and brine. While Pa ate his dinner, he spoke eagerly of what would be done before the packet sailed.

Amy marvelled at the change in her father since he became owner of the *Jenet Rae*. There was a new vigour in his step, and a pride and self-esteem she had not seen before. The packet just *had* to succeed! Not only because they would lose their home if it did not, but because, watching Pa now, Amy realised if the venture failed her father's brave heart and spirit would be broken irrevocably.

The following Sunday was harvest festival at All Hallows. Gilbert, Edmund and Collie Barraclough and his sons had spent most of the previous day driving carts around Monks Quay, collecting everything from cheeses to rush-lights and taking these gifts to the church in readiness for distribution amongst the poor and needy. Amy and Vicky had joined the womenfolk decorating the pews, pulpit, window ledges and altar with sheaves of oats, barley, wheat and hedge-row fruits.

The congregation that crisp autumnal morning was swelled by people who were not regular church-goers, and Amy felt a pang of regret for the friendship she and Dan Ainsworth had lost when she saw him arriving with his parents and younger brothers. As if sensing her gaze, he glanced across to the choir stalls and met her eyes for barely a moment before turning away and taking his seat.

Reverend Linley's simple sermon of thanks, compassion and giving was well-received by his parishioners. Gilbert's choice of music and hymns, together with his bringing the youngest members of the church to the fore during some of the singing, was a resounding contribution to All Hallows' service for the harvest festival.

The rest of Amy's day was taken up with Sunday school, helping the Reverend and Mrs Linley pack the baskets, and then lending a hand with delivering the harvest bounty all around the parish. It wasn't until the sun was setting and the sky was streaked with vivid paint-box hues that the last basket was delivered and Amy and Gilbert were finally alone, strolling back across the meadows to All Hallows.

'I suppose it's still a little early to descend upon Uncle William and Aunt Lucy,' remarked Gilbert. The vicar and his wife had invited them both for supper, but neither one was in any hurry to relinquish these precious moments.

'I'm happy just strolling and watching the sunset,' sighed Amy contentedly. 'It's been such a wonderful day!'

'A worthwhile sort of day,' agreed Gilbert, lifting her onto the sun-warmed stones of the churchyard wall and then climbing up beside her. All Hallows was built on high ground, and from their vantage point the country rolled away inland to woods and hills, and down to the shore and distant sea, the glittering water aflame with the colours of the setting sun.

'I can't help thinking . . . Oh, I don't know!' he went on edgily. 'Today I felt really *alive*, Amy! I was doing something useful. Something important. Mostly, days pass by and I haven't done anything of value at all.'

'That's not true. You're helping your father run your family's business — that's important.'

'Is it?' He held her gaze sceptically. 'I

find it increasingly meaningless.'

'It may not be worthwhile in the same way as the work your uncle does,' she argued, 'any more than my sewing and cleaning at Whiteladies Grange is as worthwhile as the work Aunt Anne does at the school; but that doesn't make what you and I do less useful.'

'I have so many privileges, I'm ashamed to be dissatisfied,' he continued soberly. 'However, more and more, I resent the Paslew family business and what's expected of me. Is that very selfish?'

'You're not your father, Gilbert. You have to make your own way in life.' She took his hands in both her own. 'Recently, Pa told us he was meant to be a coal miner like the rest of his family, but he longed to go to sea. Eventually he did.'

'I'm sorry your father disapproves of me, Amy. It must make life at home difficult for you.'

'Pa's just set in his ways. And it isn't really you he disapproves of — not you personally, I mean,' she answered frankly. 'Besides, I think he might be getting used to the notion of our being friends.'

'More than friends, I think!' Raising her hand to his lips, Gilbert touched each fingertip with a kiss. 'All the same, I don't want to cause any discord.'

'You're not!' She reached up to kiss his cheek before resting her head against his shoulder. 'I'm looking forward to seeing Fanny again, but I wish I wasn't going away to York tomorrow.'

'I don't suppose it would be wise for me to come along and see you aboard the coach.'

'Not really.' She smiled ruefully.

'We could start saying our goodbyes tonight,' he suggested, gazing down into her wide brown eyes.

'That seems sensible,' Amy responded, tilting her face to his. 'But we mustn't forget supper at the rectory . . . '

★　★　★

Although she was already missing Gilbert, Amy's spirits were high during

224

the long, uncomfortable journey from Monks Quay toward York. She was longing to see Fanny again. There'd be so much to talk about and catch up with, especially now her sister was certain she was expecting. And of course, Amy had news of her own. She couldn't wait to confide in Fanny and pour out all her innermost thoughts and feelings for Gilbert.

Nicholas Buxton was waiting patiently for her at the coaching inn when the weary horses clattered up the cobbled Shambles and around toward the Eagle and Child. Amy's first question was after Fanny's health.

'She's feeling a little better, I think,' he replied, taking Amy's portmanteau from the coachman. 'At least, she tells me so.'

He looked anxious and, it seemed to Amy, a good deal older than when she'd last seen him mere months ago. She was immediately concerned. 'What's wrong, Nick? Has something happened to Fanny? Or — or is it the baby — ?'

'No, nothing of that sort, thank God,' he instantly reassured her, adding, 'Fanny really does insist she is as well as a lady in her delicate condition might expect to be. However, she is deeply troubled — with just cause, and I am entirely responsible for her distress.'

'You?' exclaimed Amy in disbelief. 'Nick, you must explain what's going on before I see her!'

'Theo is deeply in debt, Amy. I don't know how or why it has happened. Theo seldom discusses his business affairs with me — I daresay he believes I lack sufficient brains to understand,' related Nicholas bitterly. 'The reversal in fortune seemed to occur almost overnight. We were living comfortably, then suddenly creditors were pressing to have their bills settled. Tradesmen refused to supply Cook, and lawyers' clerks were hammering at the door of Carteret Square seeking Theo. He was already gone.'

Amy's heart sank, her mind racing. Despite her certainty that she possessed a clearer picture of the nature of

Theodore's 'business' activities than her companion, she could do nothing other than listen.

'Theo told us he was going away from York for a few days in order to collect monies owed to him,' Nicholas said. 'That was almost three weeks ago.'

'Have you heard from him? Do you know where he is?'

Nicholas shook his head. 'I'm relieved you're here, Amy. I have in mind some steps I might take to ease the financial situation, but I haven't wanted to leave Fanny alone.'

'I'm very glad you've stayed with her. She must be desperately worried,' responded Amy, meeting his gaze. 'But I don't understand why you feel responsible. Theo's debts are not of your doing, Nick! You can't blame yourself for his — his imprudence!'

'It's far more than imprudence, and I do blame myself,' he returned harshly. 'I must. I've always been aware Theo sails close to the wind where money is concerned, but I've never asked for precise details of what he does. Nor ever questioned his actions.'

'You're not his keeper, Nick.'

'Perhaps I should have been! Last year, when Gilbert asked me to Whiteladies Grange as usual and Theo practically invited himself along, I should've realised he had some scheme in mind.' Taking Amy's arm, he guided her through the busy traffic and crossed Petergate toward the minster. 'Theo got along really well with Mr Paslew — far better than Gilbert does, actually. I even remember us joking about that. And I do know Mr Paslew has invested a huge amount of money in a company Theo is involved with. It's something to do with railways. Or at least, it's a company set up to build railways. Except there will never be any railways built — it's all just one great swindle!'

Amy stared at him. She'd heard of gentlemen running up debts, and she'd long believed Theodore Buxton to be unscrupulous and dishonest — suspected him of thieving and worse

— but never would she have imagined he'd be behind a fraudulent scheme of this magnitude. 'Although it does seem incredible,' she said, speaking aloud her thoughts, 'I'm sure Theodore could do something like that very easily. He's so . . . convincing.'

'Just before the wedding, I found out about the railway swindle. Confronted Theo about it. He refused to change his plans.' Nicholas added in disgust, 'He knew darn well I couldn't do anything; knew I was too weak to stand against him!'

'It's not weakness,' put in Amy soberly, recognising only too well Nicholas Buxton's dilemma. 'It's family loyalty, perhaps. I don't quite know how to describe it, but I do understand it. You wanted Theodore to tell Fanny the truth about himself, didn't you?'

Nicholas was too distracted to wonder at Amy's perspicacity. 'I was less concerned about Mr Paslew and the railway shares than about Fanny. I was pretty certain Theo had gilded the lily — exaggerated; not been honest with her. I didn't think it was fair, and I said so. I didn't want Fanny to be hurt, and now see what keeping my silence has done!'

'We'd all do things differently if we could only go back and change them,' said Amy sensibly, almost gasping at the grandeur of the tall early Georgian houses lining Carteret Square. 'Everything you've told me — does Fanny know it all?'

'She knows as much as I do,' he answered. 'Theo hasn't told either of us anything, other than to sit tight because he'll sort it all out when he comes home. I'm sorry there wasn't a carriage to meet you at the coaching inn, by the way.'

He led the way up the eight stone steps to the elegant front door, fitting his key into the brass lock. 'The servants have left, I'm afraid. Even Cook. Apparently they hadn't been given wages for quite some while.' He paused, facing Amy squarely. 'I've been so ineffectual in the past, I don't expect you to believe me when I tell you I won't let any harm come to Fanny. But I swear it!'

'I do believe you, Nick,' she murmured, her hand briefly touching his arm. 'Shall we go in?'

Fanny was much thinner than when Amy had seen her last, and her fair, creamy complexion was pinched and drawn. However, she had lost none of her spark, nor the sharp edge on her tongue.

'I do not wish to discuss Theo,' she said firmly when the sisters were drinking their tea beside the morning-room fire. 'I don't share Nicholas's disgraceful opinion of my husband. I'm convinced that whatever difficulties have arisen will be resolved the instant Theo returns.'

'Fanny! Theo's been gone three weeks without so much as a word, leaving you to face creditors!' blurted Amy, immediately wishing she'd bitten back her words. 'I'm sorry, Fan. It isn't my business.'

'No, it is not,' retorted Fanny curtly, her blue eyes glittering icily. 'Theo is my husband. I am his wife. We are soon to have a child. I am in no doubt whatsoever that when Theo returns to York, our life will continue as securely and comfortably as before. Until then, we shall manage as best we may. I'm not always able to get out and about as much as I would choose,' Fanny went on, her mood changing with the subject, 'so I am positively starved of conversation! I want to hear every scrap of news from home and Monks Quay. But first of all, you must tell me everything about Gilbert Paslew in minute detail. You're a dark horse, Amy! Stepping out with the son and heir of the richest man in Monks Quay.'

Amy lowered her eyes and sipped her tea, feeling hot colour rising to burn her cheeks.

'Well?' persisted Fanny, dabbing her temples with soothing lavender water. 'Are you really sweethearts?'

'I'm not sure what will happen between us. Pa doesn't approve, of course. And it's exactly as you say. I'm me, and he . . . well, he's Alfred Paslew's son and heir, isn't he? But Gilbert is the one, Fanny! You once told me I'd know when the right man for me came along, and I do. I love Gilbert. There can never be anyone else.'

★ ★ ★

The following morning, Nicholas took Amy aside after breakfast. 'Would you mind if I went over to Ilkley? I'll be back the day after tomorrow. We have cousins there. The children of Mother's brother. I have it in mind to ask if I might borrow some money. If I am able to repay a portion of Theo's debt, I intend visiting his creditors and trying to reason with them; perhaps keep them at bay until Theo returns and clears his obligations.'

'Of course you must go,' agreed Amy at once. 'Do you think these cousins might be able to help?'

'I'm fairly sure they have the means,' he said. 'You see, when my maternal grandfather died, he left this house and a small legacy in trust for Theo. However, he bequeathed the greater part of his estate to his son. The property in Ilkley has passed to my eldest cousin. We've met only once, when I was a boy, but we are family. He might come to our assistance.'

While Nicholas was hastily making ready for his journey, Amy cleared and washed the breakfast dishes. She was checking the huge pantry and deciding upon a light but nourishing meal for later, since she was certain Fanny wasn't eating enough, when her sister came down into the kitchen and suggested they take a stroll and explore the medieval town together.

The weather was cold but dry, and the sisters had an enjoyable day. Browsing and window-shopping, they talked and talked of anything and everything. Despite their present financial difficulties, Amy was left in no doubt that Fanny still loved Theo deeply and had not the slightest suspicion of his ruthless scheming and dishonesty.

The sisters had planned to attend evensong at the minster. However, when they returned to Carteret Square late in the afternoon, Fanny was clearly exhausted and Amy insisted she go upstairs to rest. After taking her sister a tray of tea, Amy returned to the morning-room and wrote a letter home. At Fanny's behest, she did not mention the problems at Carteret Square.

It was already growing dusk when Amy set off for the minster. It was but a short distance away, and she savoured every moment of the crisp evening air as she walked through carpets of golden and rusty leaves, swirls more of them fluttering down all about her from the old trees lining the winding path.

Evensong was an awe-inspiring, breath-taking experience. As she joined in with the ancient songs of worship, Amy's thoughts strayed again and again to Gilbert, and how very much she loved him. He'd mentioned to her that during his boyhood at school in York, he had frequently attended evensong at the minster. As she rose to sing, she smiled to think of him being here as a little boy, and allowed herself to imagine their perhaps visiting the minster together one day, as husband and wife.

It was quite dark when the service ended and Amy returned to Carteret Square. She prepared a light but sustaining supper for herself and Fanny; and after they had eaten and Fanny retired early to bed, she took her sewing-basket into the morning-room and settled down for the rest of the evening.

Lost in concentration upon the intricate embroidery and her troubled thoughts, it was very late before Amy noticed the hour and rose from the fireside for her bed. With the light held high, she walked along the dark, unfamiliar hallway, and was about to climb the staircase when she smelled smoke. It was not chimney smoke, nor was it from the range, though it did seem to emanate from the kitchen. Quickening her step, she strode down the hall and pushed open the kitchen door. Instantly, she was aware of somebody in the darkness.

'Who's there?' she demanded loudly,

her hand trembling slightly as she raised the light to better illuminate the large room. 'Who is it — *You!*'

'None other.' Rory drew on the cheroot, exhaling a plume of pungent smoke. He was sitting back in Cook's comfortable chair, his legs stretched out and propped up on the scrubbed table. 'I'm waiting to see Buxton. When do you expect him back?'

'Your guess is as good as mine.' Recovering her composure, Amy moved into the room and roughly pushed his boots from the table. For all Rory's cockiness of attitude, now that the light shone full upon him, she could see he was grimy and dishevelled. He looked exhausted, and surely that was blood staining his shirtfront and coat? 'That's if Theodore returns to York at all!'

Rory swore under his breath, wincing as he reached for the grog bottle standing before him on the table. 'How long has he been gone?'

'Almost a month.' She looked to the kitchen door. It did not appear damaged in any way, nor was the small window beside it broken. 'How did you get in? Have you a key?'

'Hardly! Buxton warned me never to come here, but needs must.' He swilled down a mouthful of liquor. 'Where's the other one — Nicholas? I saw him rushing off with a bag this morning.'

'You've been watching the house?' she exclaimed.

'Once I was sure there were no servants coming and going anymore, and young master Nicholas was out of the way, there was nowt to stop me coming in and making myself at home.'

'Why have you come here, Rory? What do you want?'

'Enough money to take me far away.'

'You're to be disappointed, for there isn't a penny piece here,' she replied briskly. 'Theodore has left his wife and household in the direst straits.'

'I'll have to rely on you helping me then.' He grinned and adding slyly, 'Of course, I could go upstairs and have a word with Fanny. Does she still believe that husband of hers is a saint? I'm sure she'd be interested to hear all about Theo's activities — and only too glad to pay me to keep my mouth shut and disappear from York!'

'You really are despicable!' Amy could not conceal her disgust. 'Fanny is unwell and worried sick besides, yet you'd destroy her just to have your own way!'

'Listen to me, Amy! I can't afford to pussyfoot around.' He leapt to his feet, confronting her. Even the spasm of pain creasing his face did not lessen the menace exuding from him. Involuntarily, Amy took a step back. 'Aye, you might well be wary! I'm a wanted man. And if I get caught, I swear to God that before I dance at the end of the rope, I'll shop Theodore Buxton and take him down with me. So if you don't want to make Fanny a widow and her unborn babe a fatherless orphan, you'll do exactly what I tell you!'

Amy's legs felt weak at the knees, and she gripped the table edge to steady herself. 'Lord above, Rory — whatever have you done?'

'Does it matter?'

'What have you *done*?' she repeated, indicating his bloodstained shirt and coat. 'How were you wounded?'

'I was delivering some goods, if you must know. The bloke baulked at paying what he owed. We had a tussle and he got me with his blade. I laid into him. He went down hard on the cobbles. Didn't get up.'

'You've *killed* a man?'

'I don't know. If I did, I didn't mean to. It was an accident.' Rory met her gaze, and Amy saw the stark fear in her brother's narrowed eyes. 'Folk were coming and I had to get away. Didn't have time to take the money or anything. I just ran for it.'

Amy stared at him. 'From your outward appearance, you and Theodore Buxton are as different as two men might be. Beneath the surface, you are as alike as two peas in a pod! Both of you survive on your wits and live by guile and deceit instead of honest labour.' Now anger and frustration were flaring within her. 'Both of you trample all before you, with neither conscience nor loyalty nor scruple for those who care most for you!'

'For all your sermonising, you'll do as I say, Amy,' Rory remarked, all trace of fear now gone from his countenance. 'Besides, like I told you, it was an accident. I'm innocent.'

'I don't know whether to believe this tale of yours or not. My conscience already troubles me for my part in helping you evade justice in Monks Quay,' she snapped. 'I will help you, Rory, as you knew I would. But know also, it is not because of the liar, thief and — heaven forbid — the murderer I now see before me, but for the dear brother you once were so very long ago. You might have become so again,' she said despairingly, 'if only you had been strong enough to mend your ways and work hard to lead a decent, honest life!'

'Like Pa, you mean? Breaking my

back grafting to line another man's pockets?' he retaliated scornfully. 'I'd rather take my chances than end up like Pa — bowed and broken and still scratching for pennies as the feet of the likes of Alfred Paslew!'

'If you survive a thousand years, you'll never be a tenth of the man Pa is!'

'Maybe.' He shrugged, placing the grog in his pocket and starting past her from the kitchen into the hall.

'Where are you going?'

'Reckon I'll take myself up to one of them nice soft beds upstairs — I've not had a decent sleep in a while.' He grinned down at Amy's alarmed face. 'I'll try not to disturb Fanny. Not yet awhile, anyhow. Oh, you won't forget about that money I need, will you?'

'I've told you. There's no money here.'

'There's plenty as might be sold.'

'I can't sell Fanny's household belongings!'

'You'll be surprised at what you can do, little sister! I'll pick out a bagful of stuff and you'll take it to the pop shop.

Couldn't be easier,' he said, lighting another smoke from her candle and starting upstairs. 'And remember, the quicker you get my money, the sooner I'll be gone and leaving you and her ladyship in peace!'

*　*　*

On the day of Amy's departure from York, Fanny insisted upon accompanying her and Nicholas to the coaching inn. They walked arm in arm along Petersgate, talking nineteen to the dozen. For all her present adversity and delicate condition, Fanny's temperament had lost none of its sharpness.

'My blood still boils whenever I think of Rory barging into my home — my home! — demanding money to get himself out of trouble!' she fumed. 'How dare he! I can never thank you enough for handling everything so discreetly, Amy. Especially the pawnbroker. When I imagine the scandal that worthless brother so nearly caused . . . ' Fanny shuddered in disgust, her head high and her blue eyes glinting. 'Transportation and years of hard labour would be far too good for him — I'd certainly have had plenty to say to him, had *I* found him in the kitchen that night!'

'There's been enough for you to contend with of late, without that,' replied Amy, choosing her next words carefully, for even the slightest criticism of Theodore Buxton antagonised her sister. 'Now that Nicholas has spoken to some of the creditors, hopefully they'll not be quite so troublesome. For a while, at least.'

'There's no cause for you to mention my present plight to the family, Amy,' instructed Fanny, when the sisters were hugging goodbye at the coach. 'All will be set to rights when Theo arrives home.'

9

A north-easterly wind had whipped the tide into deep, spume-flecked furrows upon the grey wintry morning Ramsay Macfarlene set sail. The *Jenet Rae* was heavily laden, and Ramsay had ambitiously planned a much longer trip than usual. As the chill days became shorter and weeks slipped by, Amy tried to picture the packet's arduous journey, often wondering where exactly the *Jenet Rae* might be. She unearthed one of Pa's old charts and she and Vicky plotted the packet's course as best they could: up to Furness, across to the Isle of Man and on to Ireland, over to Liverpool, and then the little boat would hug the ragged Lancashire coast northwards all the way home to Monks Quay.

Despite winter's tightening grip upon the woods and fields, the weather had not yet taken a serious turn for the worse, and there was no reason to suppose Pa would not be ashore in plenty of time for Christmas. Amy had made the plum puddings and started her Christmas baking soon after returning from York. It seemed very lonely making all the festive recipes without Fanny at her side, organising every last detail, and she found herself wondering again and again what sort of Christmas her elder sister would celebrate this year. At least Fanny's regular letters were now bringing more hopeful news. Her health was greatly improved. Theodore was back, and life at Carteret Square appeared to have settled into a comfortable routine once more. Neverthetheless, reading between the lines, Amy couldn't quell the suspicion that all was far from well with her brother-in-law's financial activities.

'It was very frosty last night and all the stars were really bright,' Vicky was saying, holding the tin tightly while Amy carefully spooned the mixture into it. The sisters had spent the morning finishing off the Christmas baking, and this light, festive fruitcake from Ma's very own recipe was always the last thing to be made. 'So the Dog Star will be sparklier than ever, won't it? Pa'll easily see his way home! He did say he might be back this week, didn't he?'

'Yes, but you know Pa can never promise, Vicky,' cautioned Amy, smoothing the surface of the mixture. 'Now he's the owner of the *Jenet Rae*, he's got an awful lot of extra work to do during this trip; folk he has to meet and talk to and make business arrangements with. And besides, there hasn't been much wind. If there isn't enough wind to fill the sails,' she said as she gave Vicky the mixing bowl to scrape out, 'the packet can't sail.'

Once the cake was safely in the oven, Amy took off her apron and made ready to follow the family's yuletide tradition. 'Vicky and I are off up to St Agnes Falls to make the Christmas wishes,' she said, popping her head into the sitting-room where Edmund was studying. 'Are you coming? We're taking a winter picnic.'

'I have to finish this Latin paper for when Gilbert comes round tonight,' he replied, adding innocently, 'I asked him to stay for supper. You don't mind, do you?'

Amy's romance with Gilbert was blossoming, but she threw her brother a haughty glance and flounced out. 'Back to your studies, my lad!'

St Agnes Falls lay hidden deep in the heart of Friars Wood. Amy and Vicky could hear the soft whisper and splash of the ancient spring tumbling down over mossy stones a good while before they entered the dell with its overgrown ivy, holly and pagan mistletoe. Despite the brilliant sunshine pouring down through the leafless branches of tall trees, patches of glittering white frost were still crisp in the shady nooks and corners surrounding the falls.

Holding tightly onto Vicky's hand, Amy gazed all about her in wonder.

There was something so very special and magical about this beautiful, tranquil place, especially at this time of year. The sisters silently cast their Christmas wishes before the sparkling waters of the spring. Amy's wish was always the same, though this year she added special words for Gilbert.

Wrapped up warmly against the cold, she and Vicky found a sunny spot for their picnic of sliced bun loaf and toasted beechnuts. Afterwards, while Vicky and her rag doll were collecting the last of the year's sweet chestnuts, Amy took the opportunity to settle down and write to Fanny. It was Vicky who first heard approaching hoofbeats, and a moment or two later horse and rider walked into the glade.

'Gilbert!' exclaimed Amy in surprise. 'How did you know we were here?'

'I didn't.' He dismounted, and she immediately sensed his dejection. 'It's so peaceful, I always come here whenever I need to get away and think. I've been working with my father all day. Well, arguing would be more accurate. I can't imagine how he expects us to work side by side productively when we never can agree about anything.'

'It's such a shame, Gilbert,' Amy murmured sympathetically.

He came to her side, staring deep into the crystal-clear waters of St Agnes Falls. 'I wish things were different, Amy. I have tried these past months, I truly have. However, my being part of the family business is never going to work. Father and I view things so very differently.'

'Couldn't you both compromise?'

'*Compromise* is not within my father's vocabulary,' he replied briskly. 'For my part, well, I believe there are certain basic principles that must be observed, regardless of the figures on a balance-sheet.'

'It seems as though the pair of you have at least one trait in common!'

Gilbert smiled in spite of his dismal mood. 'Father and I do get along fairly well. It's only when 'Paslew and Son' rears its mercenary head that we're constantly at odds.'

'What will you do?'

'I'm not certain, and that's a huge part of the problem.' He met her eyes despairingly. 'When I was at Oxford, everything seemed so very clear. I had such a sure sense of direction; of what my future would be. I need to find that certainty again, Amy.'

Alarm shot through her. 'You're not going to leave Monks — '

'Amy!'

She and Gilbert were instantly on their feet and across the dell. Vicky was sitting amongst the crinkled leaves, nursing her foot and looking very sorry for herself.

'What happened?' Amy asked her.

'I climbed up the trunk to get that chestnut.' She pointed to a solitary nut left on the old tree. 'And I slipped!'

'You're supposed to gather chestnuts from the ground, not climb up and pick them off the tree!' said Amy, gently feeling the little girl's ankle and foot. 'No bones broken. We'll go home and put a cold compress on your ankle so it won't swell too much.'

'You both can ride,' Gilbert said, fetching the bay mare. 'Whiteladies is nearest — we'll be there in no time.'

Vicky was unusually bashful and tongue-tied when she was sitting in the drawing-room at Whiteladies Grange, gazing wide-eyed all around her. She'd never seen such a room before, nor imagined a room could be so big and filled with so many grand things. Amy quickly bathed and bound her sister's bruised ankle, and at Gilbert's insistence, a tray of hot chocolate and shortbread was sent for from the kitchen.

'Chocolate and shortbread are essential whenever you fall out of a tree,' he told Vicky. 'There's no finer remedy — ask any physician!'

The three were finishing off their chocolate, and Amy was explaining her plans for Sunday school activities during the remaining weeks of Advent, when the drawing-room door swung open and Alfred Paslew stood on the threshold.

'I beg your pardon,' he murmured curtly, his astute gaze considering the scene before he turned into the hallway once more and noiselessly closed the door.

Alfred Paslew had not displayed any disapproval, though Amy sensed the unspoken censure. That evening at Clockmakers Cottage, after supper was over and Gilbert had gone home, she worried lest her and Vicky's presence in the drawing-room at Whiteladies would provoke yet another row between father and son.

Upon her arrival at Whiteladies Grange long before first light the following morning, Amy was confronted by the cold expression of Alfred Paslew's displeasure the instant she scurried into the kitchen.

Gladys Braithwaite turned from the range to face her, pushing a dish of coins across the kitchen table. 'Don't trouble to take off your coat! You've been let go.' The cook pursed her lips. 'I'm to give you your wages till the month's end. You're lucky to get them, considering!'

Amy stared at Mrs Braithwaite in disbelief. 'I've — I've lost my place?'

'I'm only surprised you got away with it as long as you did!'

'Got away with — '

'Don't come the innocent, miss! You know full well what I mean! Making up to Mr Gilbert like you have been!' she went on. 'Your Fanny did well for herself, marrying a gent and all, and I daresay you thought you'd do the same. You played with fire, my girl, and now you've got your fingers burned good and proper!'

Amy just stood, sick to her stomach and too shocked even to defend herself. She wanted to turn on her heel and march away; refuse to scoop the coins from the dish. But her family needed every penny far too badly for her to have the luxury of pride. Unable to speak, and with tears perilously close, she gathered up her wages and walked straight-backed from the kitchen. Once beyond that door, all she wanted was to get away from Whiteladies Grange as fast as she could.

'Amy! Wait!' a low voice hissed from the shadows of the backstairs. Clemmie

Paslew stepped out into the passageway and hugged her impulsively. 'It's awful, Amy! Just awful! Father shouldn't have done this. It's not fair! Mamma is dreadfully upset. So are Sophie and me. And Gilbert will be furious when he finds out!'

Mist was seeping up from the sea, and Amy's hair and clothing were shrouded with dampness when she returned to Clockmakers Cottage. Placing the money in the tea caddy, she sank onto one of the kitchen chairs, still wearing her cloak and bonnet. She'd been fortunate to receive wages from Whiteladies, but even so . . .

Edmund clattered down the stairs, dressed ready to go out. 'What are you doing here?' he asked her. 'What's wrong?'

She told him. 'At least the family won't be any worse off, not until the end of the month. After that, well, I just don't know how we'll manage!'

'Pa will be home shortly,' replied Edmund optimistically, 'with the proceeds of his first voyage.'

'He has that huge debt to repay. We need every farthing.' Amy's fingers knotted and unknotted in her lap. 'What am I going to do, Teddy? Wherever will I find another place?'

'The weeks before Christmas are busy everywhere. Someone is bound to need an extra pair of hands,' he replied, adding after a moment's thought, 'Jessup's! Mr Jessup is looking for an assistant.'

She nodded dismally. 'I saw the card advertising the position in Mr Jessup's window, but I haven't any experience of working in a shop.'

'You can read and write and do arithmetic,' he persisted. 'You love books and writing letters. You're the ideal stationer's assistant!'

'I was dismissed, Teddy! Dismissed without references! Do you really believe a reputable businessman like Mr Jessup would trust me to serve in his shop? Monks Quay is a small town, and folk are bound to gossip about my losing my place at Whiteladies Grange so suddenly. Without a good character, what hope have I of ever securing another post?'

'Perhaps *I* should apply for the position at Jessup's,' he suggested at length. 'If I had a proper job, as well as helping out at the Mermaid — '

'No,' Amy said decisively, standing to face him. 'Absolutely not. The hopes of our whole family rest with you and your doing well in life. The scholarship examinations are in a couple of months; you mustn't throw away all your hard work now.'

'We'll see,' was Edmund's only reply as he took his coat from the back of the door and left the house.

⋆   ⋆   ⋆

It had been a long, dismal day, and the afternoon was already closing in to dusk when Amy finished pressing Vicky's pinafores and set the heavy flat-irons to cool on the hob. Clockmakers Cottage was shadowy and silent. Even the tide and the seabirds were subdued and distant. Amy had kept busy, but she felt restless and distracted. Her mind was weary, ragged with dwelling upon what had occurred and worrying about what would become of her now. She almost cried out for joy when she heard the click of the gate and saw Gilbert striding up the path. Instantly she flew into his arms.

'I am so sorry, Amy! It's disgraceful, and utterly unjust!' He held her tightly, pressing his lips to her forehead. 'Are you all right?'

She nodded, drawing comfort from the strength of his embrace. 'Did — did you quarrel with your father? About me, I mean?'

'He had neither the grace nor the decency to even mention his actions!' returned Gilbert furiously. 'We breakfasted together, and he said not a word! But for Clemmie finding me at the stables and explaining what Father had done, I wouldn't have known! So I confronted him. I still find it difficult to accept that my own father could behave so shamefully.' He distractedly pushed a hand through his damp hair. 'I can't bear to look at him, much less work at his side!'

Shaken by the violence of Gilbert's emotions, the consequences of his words only gradually dawned upon Amy. 'No, Gilbert, you can't do this. Not on my account — '

'It isn't because of you, Amy,' he said gently, his wrath abating. 'I should have taken this step earlier. I can no longer be party to my father's ruthless ambition, or remain under his roof.'

'You've left Whiteladies? It's your home, Gilbert!' she exclaimed in horror. 'This is all my fault, isn't it? It's because — '

'It's because my father and I have different values,' he interrupted quietly.

'Where will you go?' She drew him inside to the warmth of the fireside, taking his wet cloak. 'You — you'd be welcome to stay here for a few days.'

'Thank you, but it wouldn't be wise,' he replied at once. 'I shan't stay at the rectory either, although I'm sure my aunt and uncle would offer me a bed. I don't wish to create friction between them and Father; he has little enough time for Uncle William as it is. No, I came straight here from Whiteladies, and until I've made my plans, I'll put up at the Mermaid Inn.'

'The Mermaid?' Amy echoed, looking round from putting the tea kettle to boil.

'There really isn't anywhere else in Monks Quay,' he said, adding as an afterthought, 'If you'd prefer I didn't stay there . . . I know you and Dan Ainsworth were very close once. I wouldn't want to cause any further difficulties for you, Amy.'

'You won't!' She smiled, fetching cups and saucers. 'Dan and I were old friends from childhood. Even though we don't have much to say to one another these days, he and his family are still good friends and neighbours of ours.'

'I don't suppose I'll be at the Mermaid for very long, anyway,' Gilbert remarked, drawing her onto his lap.

'What are you going to do?' she

murmured fearfully, her face close to his. 'Will — will you go back to Oxford?'

'I probably need some guidance from Vicky's Dog Star!' He smiled ruefully. 'All I'm certain of is that I mean to earn my own living. Since I'm no longer working for my father, I'll not rely upon his wealth either. It's immoral to be a gentleman of leisure when women and children are forced into virtual slavery in mines and mills to avoid starvation. I have to build my own future, Amy. As every man should.' He stared past her, into the glowing coals of the fire. 'But first, I must be absolutely sure the direction I'm taking is the best one.'

★   ★   ★

A horde of terrors visited Amy that night, keeping her from sleep and tormenting her with fears for Pa somewhere out at sea, for Edmund and Vicky, for the sea-worthiness of the *Jenet Rae* and the security of their home, and for the bleakness of her own prospects. Still more dominant during those long hours of wakefulness were Amy's anguished thoughts about Gilbert. Although he hadn't yet made any decisions, he was going to leave Monks Quay; she was certain about that.

She tossed and turned, exhausted, yet denied rest. She'd understood how shocked and distressed Gilbert had been yesterday afternoon, however only now did she realise he'd scarcely mentioned her dismissal from Whiteladies Grange, or the desperate plight it put her in. He'd spoken at length about many things, but not once of Amy or the affection and attachment they shared. In the cold, lonely hours before dawn, she stared wide-eyed into the darkness, agonising whether the direction and future Gilbert sought included her. Or had she already lost him?

After taking Vicky to school, Amy gathered a trug of fresh evergreens and went into All Hallows. She was arranging the glossy greenery when the west door opened and Eleanor Paslew came inside, her footsteps soft upon the stone flags.

'Good morning, Amy.' She smiled hesitantly. 'I was on my way to visit you at Clockmakers Cottage and saw you coming into the church. However, if you're busy . . . '

'Not at all, Mrs Paslew!' she replied, returning the smile. 'The Erskines' new baby is being christened this morning. It's such a dreary day, I thought a few evergreens around the font and pews might make it all a bit brighter and more cheerful.'

'You're a very thoughtful young woman, Amy. I'm deeply sorry to lose you from Whiteladies Grange,' said Eleanor Paslew quietly. 'I believe you're aware of the high regard my daughters and I have for you. I hope this might prove useful.'

Extending a gloved hand, the older woman offered a letter addressed *To Whom It May Concern*. Inwardly, Amy heaved an enormous sigh of relief. It could only be a character reference! This would be invaluable for her prospects of securing respectable employment.

'Thank you, ma'am.'

'It's owed to you, Amy. I wonder if you might do me a favour? You may recall our measuring for new curtains for the drawing and dining rooms and Mr Paslew's study?'

Amy nodded. 'I wrote out the order and posted it to Mosley's last week.'

'Would you consider making the curtains for me? Splendid!' Mrs Paslew's smile reached her eyes now, lighting her plain features. 'As soon as the material arrives from Liverpool, I'll have it brought out to you at Clockmakers Cottage. Meanwhile, if you'd continue doing the regular weekly sewing for Whiteladies, I'd be very much obliged.'

Amy's spirits were soaring as she swiftly finished arranging the foliage. She'd been given a glowing reference, had regular work sewing for Whiteladies, would have the huge job of making the curtains and, most importantly of all, Eleanor Paslew clearly did not disapprove of Amy's friendship with her son!

Leaving All Hallows, Amy went to

find Gilbert at the Mermaid Inn, taking some pains to avoid bumping into Dan Ainsworth. She was aware he still had tender feelings for her, and was anxious not to hurt him more than she already had.

'Are you sure you want to do this immediately?' queried Gilbert, when the pair were striding arm-in-arm down Abbotsgate.

'Absolutely! Thanks to your mother, I have a wonderful reference, and I'm going to ask Mr Jessup if he'll take me on as his assistant!'

'In your present mood, he won't dare refuse!' They'd reached the crooked little stationer's with its windows filled with books and paint boxes. 'I'll wait for you in Miss Bower's tearoom.'

Gilbert was actually waiting on the street outside Jessup's when Amy emerged triumphant. 'I start straight away!'

'Hadn't you better go back inside then?'

'Not straight away this minute,' she giggled. 'First thing tomorrow morning.'

'Then we must make the most of today,' he declared, taking her arm. 'Coffee and almond tarts at Miss Bower's to celebrate?'

They were settling into their usual secluded little corner table when the tiny brass bell above the tearoom's low door jangled violently and banged back against its hinges. Ned Yarkin stood in the doorway, framed by the gloom of the afternoon without.

'Amy, lass — I've already seen Teddy. He said ye'd likely be here.' The old man struggled to get his breath. 'I were down on the shore, collecting coal. I spotted her with my spyglass — the *Jenet Rae* — ' He broke off as the bells of All Hallows commenced urgent tolling, and Amy's blood was suddenly ice water in her veins. She grasped the elderly man's trembling hands. 'Aye, she's in trouble, lass.'

With the melancholy peal of the bells loud in her ears, Amy raced down the cobbled streets from the town to the shore, heedless of Gilbert's bidding for her wait while he fetched horses. Other folk were running too, alerted by the church bells to a peril on the sea.

It was a dull day and the darkest time of year, and the already poor light was fading fast when Amy reached the hard, damp sand. She strained her eyes to penetrate the grey murkiness, scanning the vast distance before her. She could see nothing.

'Perhaps Mr Yarkin was mistaken,' suggested Gilbert softly.

'I've been praying for that be true, but if Ned Yarkin says it's so, then it is,' she answered. 'Before he became pot-man at the Mermaid, he sailed the seas for sixty years and more. He wouldn't make a mistake about a vessel in distress. There! There she is!' An indistinct grey blur pitched and rolled against a grey sky and even greyer sea.

'Here, lass.' Ned pushed the spyglass into her cold hands. 'Take a look. Ah! Here comes Teddy.'

Amy turned to see Edmund arriving onto the shore with Dan Ainsworth and his brothers. There must have been a score more people besides: men, women and children clustered in tight little groups, watching the drama unfolding before them.

'Is she going to go down?' Amy's question was directed at Ned.

'What is it that's gone wrong?' put in Gilbert, also to the elderly man.

'Wind's wrong, and there's not tide enough to bring her in,' Ned told them as he squinted out across the indolent rise and fall of the slate-grey water, now punctured by a ramrod-straight barrage of rain. 'Your pa's only chance is to bring her through the gulley to the pool, drop anchor and bide his time. He'll have to be quick about it, though,' said the old man morosely, 'or the ebb'll take him straight onto Judas Rock, and the packet'll go the way of many another boat before her!'

'What's happening, Mr Yarkin?' asked Edmund desperately. 'Where are the gulley and pool? Is Pa doing what you said?'

'Dun't seem to be doing owt. She's not making any way,' he muttered, taking back the spyglass and focussing upon the tiny vessel. 'The gulley's hard to find at best, and from that distance in this light, your pa'll scarce be able to see shore at all.' Ned turned to those standing around the shore, and suddenly the crotchety old pot-man who was the butt of many a joke had every man's undivided attention. 'Split up, lads. Half of you go up to Fiddler's Pike and t'other out to Smedley's Mill. Take torches — anything you can get that'll keep alight in this wet. And make sure you do keep 'em alight — the lives of every man aboard that boat are depending on it!'

'Edmund's going to Fiddler's Pike, and I'll head up to the mill,' murmured Gilbert, his arm protectively about Amy's shoulders. 'Unless you'd rather I stayed? I really don't like leaving you alone.'

'I'll be all right. Mr Yarkin's here,' she whispered brokenly. 'I only wish I could do something, instead of standing here watching and waiting!'

Hugging her tightly, Gilbert went from her side and disappeared amongst the throng of men and boys streaming with all speed back up to town.

'Do ye know owt about the gulley, lass?' asked Ned when they were left alone. 'No? I'm not surprised. It's a canny stretch of water. Leads between the sandbanks into a deep pool that's safe anchorage, whatever the tide. Three fathoms it is, even at low water. Once yer pa gets there, he'll be safe as houses.'

Amy didn't feel the cold, but couldn't stop shivering. 'Why have the men gone out with torches?'

'Ah, the pool isn't buoyed! When ye're out at sea, the only sure guide in to harbour is to line up two landmarks — Fiddler's Pike and Smedley's Mill, which is down-coast. If you stick to that line — and it's a tight 'un — you can sail nice and easy between the seaward sandbank and the landward sandbank straight into the pool's deep water. But in this dusk and with the rain and all, Ramsay won't be able to see the landmarks. Torches will light 'em up grand, so yer pa'll spot 'em no trouble!'

'Like beacons?' Amy got out through chattering teeth. 'I understand now. Thank you — for everything, Mr Yarkin.'

The old man stood with her a while longer before shuffling away, and she absently heard him talking to Dan Ainsworth, who'd brought down the wagon. She half-turned and caught the exchange of a glance between the two men that filled her with dread. Despite Ned's encouraging talk, was the *Jenet Rae* already a lost cause?

Presently, Dan came over to where she was standing. 'Here, wrap yourself up in this oilskin,' he murmured, draping the garment about her. 'Is there owt you want me to do, Amy?'

She met his concerned eyes and shook her head. He waited with her. They saw the procession of torches moving along to Smedley's Mill and snaking upwards to Fiddler's Pike, and waited.

'Here she comes!' Ned's shout went up. He passed his spyglass to Amy. 'Yer pa's seen the torches and he's taking her through the gulley!'

Amy held the glass to her eye, hardly able to watch, yet unable to tear her gaze from the tiny boat inching its way through perilous, churning waters.

'He's taking it steady. That's good. He durn't rush,' muttered Ned, more to himself than anyone else. 'Them sand-banks are shifting all the time. Ramsay'll be watching the torches and keeping his eye on the water below at the same time.'

It was nearly dark and the wind was freshening. Amy's gaze was fixed upon the *Jenet Rae*. She heard Dan's exclamation.

'Ned — the torches!'

She raised her face, following their eyes. The lights on Fiddler's Pike were guttering, all but extinguished by the gusting rain.

'Let's hope the lads get 'em going again quick-smart,' Ned muttered, raising the spyglass and looking seaward once more. 'I reckon there's not much further to the pool and — she's drifting off course!'

Amy snatched the glass, but could see nothing. She handed it back to Ned, unable to speak.

One glance was as much as the old seaman needed. Amy heard his shuddering breath. 'She's gone — run aground on the landward bank!'

The stillness and tension of the past hours exploded into noise and activity. Ned was yelling orders and folk were running in all directions.

'Amy! Amy, listen to me!' Dan Ainsworth shook her hard, jolting her back from shock. 'Ned says the waves aren't running high or strong enough to break her up. We're putting out rowboats, and we'll bring your da and the crew ashore. Why don't you go home to your aunt and Vicky? There's nowt you can do here.'

She shook her head.

'Have it your own way. Stay close to Ned. I'm fetching down the boat now. Da and me'll row out as soon as we're able.'

Finding her voice at last, Amy clutched both his hands. 'Dan — please be careful!'

He stood stock-still, and Amy recognised the emotion behind his eyes. Then the moment passed. He touched a hand to her cold cheek and sprinted up the shore towards the boat-house.

The sky was completely dark, the only light from torches burning at the two landmarks, when Dan and his father pushed their rowboat out into the lapping black water. Scrambling aboard when she was afloat, they lit their lantern and took the oars, pulling hard to make headway. Three other boats followed their lead. From the shore, all that could be seen was the flickering of the lanterns like so many darting fireflies in the void of night. Soon even they disappeared, and there was just darkness and the soft rush and whisper of the distant sea.

At long last, pinpoints of lantern-light appeared again. 'Coming ashore!' The call was barely audible through the rain, but loud enough for those waiting to wade into the shallows ready to grab the rowboats when they drew near and haul them up onto the safety of the shore.

Collie Barraclough's sons were first, their boat dragged clear of the water by onlookers. One glance told Amy that Pa was not among the three men rescued. The next boat was empty, save for the rowers. The last two came in together. Jim Erskine sat doubled up in one, and a cry escaped Amy's lips when she saw only Dan and his father aboard the other.

'Take it easy, lass!' Dan leapt over the side and caught her as she floundered through the shallows, peering down into the boat. 'Your da's passed out. His leg's got hurt, but he's alive!'

Ramsay lay white and still, his leg bloody and torn. She watched Dan and his father lift him from the boat and put him carefully into the wagon.

'We nearly made it, Miss Macfarlene,' said one of the packet's crewmen as he passed. 'A right shame, it was. The sandbank got us at t'end!'

'I'm glad you're safe,' she managed to say. 'What — what about Jim Erskine?'

'Bad, miss. I don't know what happened, but he's in a right mess.'

'There'll be food and a few tots at the Mermaid,' Dan called to the crewman, whose name Amy didn't know. 'Harry Smedley will take you up there in his cart. Oh, and . . . ' He moved from Amy's hearing and she leaned into the wagon, bundling the blankets closer around her father. She started when Gilbert was suddenly beside her, with Teddy just a short distance behind.

'Ned Yarkin told me they got all the crew off safely,' he said earnestly. 'You must — '

'This is your father's fault!' She glared at him, her fingers gripping the edge of the wagon. 'He'd neglected the packet.

Hadn't repaired her. The *Jenet Rae* was barely seaworthy when your father sold her to mine. And because Pa isn't rich like your father, he risked his life on a dangerous voyage so he could pay his way and provide for his family! If it wasn't for Ned, Pa and the crew could've died tonight!' Her voice was shaking. 'Do you realise that, Gilbert? Pa and the others might've drowned, and it would've been your family's fault!'

Dan strode across to the wagon and swung up onto the seat next to Edmund. 'Amy, we need to get your da home. There's no time to hang about.'

Grasping the hand he extended, she clambered up beside him, leaving Gilbert standing alone as the wagon pulled away towards Clockmakers Cottage.

* * *

Hours later, when Ramsay was sleeping easily on the bed Amy had made up for him in the sitting-room, she tiptoed out into the kitchen. Edmund looked worn out, but he sat at the table still, his head bowed over his books.

'You should be in bed, not studying.'

'Couldn't sleep if I did go up,' he replied. 'I can't concentrate on this either, but it's better than thinking about what might have happened to Pa and the crew.'

'Oh, Teddy.' She sat across from him, burying her face into her hands. 'I thought we'd lost him!'

'I heard Mr Ainsworth saying the packet would've swept onto the Judas Rocks and been smashed to matchwood, but for Ned Yarkin,' murmured Edmund soberly. 'He always seems so old and muddled, yet he knew everything about the gulley and the landmarks. And it was his idea to go up with torches. He saved them all, didn't he?'

'Yes, he did. We've a lot to be thankful for this night.' She sighed. 'Pa's leg will heal with time, but Doctor Tadman said Jim Erskine might lose his arm. It was badly crushed when the packet ran aground. His baby was christened today.

What sort of Christmas will that family have? How will they manage, if Jim is crippled for life?'

Edmund studied her pinched face before speaking. 'What you said to Gilbert about the *Jenet Rae* — it might've been true, but it wasn't Gilbert's fault, Amy. None of this is his responsibility.'

'You're right,' she admitted unhappily. 'I don't know what came over me. I was so angry and frightened. I still feel frightened, and I don't even know why. Pa's safe, and it's all over, yet I still have this . . . this awful fear inside me, and it isn't going away. I want to cry all the time.'

'You need to get some sleep. When you see Gilbert again, everything will be all right. He'll have understood. Go on up to bed, Amy. I'll sit with Pa in case he wakes.'

* * *

'Edmund tells me you're starting a new job today,' remarked Ramsay when Amy took his breakfast into the sitting-room. 'I never cared much for you skivvying for the likes of them up at Whiteladies Grange. Selling books and suchlike at Jessup's is a big step up in the world.'

'Mrs Paslew did give me a very good character, Pa, and she's sending sewing for me to do here at home.'

'Eleanor Paslew's a decent enough woman, I suppose. Your aunt thinks highly of her. Shouldn't you be getting along to your new job?'

'Not today, Pa.'

'Why not? Because of me? I may have a gammy leg, but I'm not a helpless invalid!' he retorted. 'Nay, lass — you go off to Jessup's. I'll be glad of some time to myself. I've a deal of thinking to do.'

Amy's first days working at the stationer's were demanding, with many new things to learn and remember. She had to concentrate so hard upon her various duties that there wasn't time to dwell upon her family's troubles or her harsh words to Gilbert. Amy hadn't seen or heard from him since the *Jenet Rae* had run aground. She was aware he and Teddy had taken to meeting at the schoolhouse for their study sessions.

How swiftly everything had changed! Just one week ago, she'd felt such great happiness and contentment whenever she and Gilbert were together. Even being apart had a sweet longing, and she'd dreamt of them being together always. Then that afternoon at St Agnes Falls when he'd spoken about returning to Oxford, Amy's dreams had been shot through with doubt.

Had Gilbert ever loved her, *really* loved her? fretted Amy as she walked from Jessup's towards Clockmakers Cottage. Or did he merely care for her, in a similar manner as she cared for Dan Ainsworth? Was this constant pain and sadness deep inside her how Dan had felt when she had refused his proposal? Was the awful, aching emptiness how it felt to love somebody completely and not have that love requited? Amy bowed her head against the sea wind, quickening her steps home.

The Ainsworths' wagon was drawn into the sheltered side of Clockmakers Cottage, and when Amy went indoors she found Dan, Ned and Teddy gathered in the sitting-room with her father. Pa was in his favourite armchair, his leg propped on a stool and a sturdy stick at his side.

'It seems Ned and Dan went out to the *Jenet Rae* the day after she foundered, saved what cargo they could and collected the money for it,' explained Ramsay with a broad grin. 'Ned reckons that although the boat took a beating, she's not beyond repair, and once she's patched up she should fetch a bob or two.'

'That's wonderful, Pa!' Amy looked from Ned to Dan. 'Thank you both. You've — excuse me, I'll just see who's at the door.'

'Could be Collie Barraclough and Da,' called Dan after her. 'They said they'd follow us up here.'

However, when Amy opened the front door, it wasn't Collie Barraclough and Mr Ainsworth standing before her, but Gilbert Paslew. 'Hello, Amy,' he spoke diffidently, not moving toward her. 'I came to ask after your father. And yourself.'

'He's on the mend,' she mumbled uncomfortably. 'Thank you for asking.'

'And yourself? I've been concerned, but I didn't want to . . . That is, I thought it might perhaps be best to wait awhile. I called at Jessup's this evening, in the hope of meeting you when you left the shop, but you'd already gone.'

'Mr Jessup has been very kind, letting me leave a little early each evening.' She raised her eyes, meeting his steadily. 'Gilbert, I'm so very sorry for what I said on the shore. I — '

'That terrible night is over, Amy,' he gently interrupted. 'Have you heard about Jim Erskine? Dr Tadman managed to save his arm.'

'Thank goodness! Have you seen him yourself?'

'Yes, my uncle and I visited his family earlier today. The other three crewmen are doing well, too. It was Jim and your father who were most badly hurt.' He glanced to the wagon standing beside the cottage. 'You have visitors. This obviously isn't a convenient time, but I need to talk to you about my plans. Can we meet later this evening? Or tomorrow, perhaps?' He reached for her hand but Amy jerked back, pulling free as though burned.

'I — I don't ... ' she flustered, shocked at the flame of emotion his glancing touch provoked. Her heart was hammering, hot colour flooding her face. She read the rejection and confusion in Gilbert's clear eyes, yet could only stare wordlessly at him, desperately wanting him to take her into his arms.

'Amy!' Dan Ainsworth emerged from the sitting-room into the unlit kitchen behind her. 'Are you coming back in?'

'Yes, I'm coming,' she mumbled mechanically without turning around. She was gazing up into Gilbert's face, and what she saw there overwhelmed her with longing and loss. He *didn't* love her! He was going to leave her. That was what he'd come to tell her. And Amy knew she couldn't bear to hear him say it. She swallowed hard, lowering her eyes. 'I'd better go in. Pa and the others are waiting.'

'Yes, I can see that,' he returned coldly. 'I just wanted you to know I'm leaving for Oxford.'

'When?' she heard herself ask.

'Aboard the next southbound coach.'

'How long will you be gone?'

'I'm not yet certain.'

'You won't leave Monks Quay for good!' She lifted her eyes, only to flinch against his hostile expression.

'There isn't any reason for me to stay.' He turned away down the path, pausing with his hand on the gate to look back at her. 'Goodbye, Amy.'

A silent cry choked Amy's throat. She gulped in a deep breath, fighting the wild impulse to run after Gilbert and beg him not to go. Instead, she stood shivering on the doorstep. Tears of grief stung her eyes as she watched him mount his horse, and ride away without a backward glance.

Then Dan was beside her once more. She followed him into the kitchen and lit the lamps.

It had ended.

10

Amy missed Gilbert most of all on Sundays. She missed hearing his tenor voice singing in the choir stalls just a few feet behind her; seeing him come into All Hallows when the children had gone home and she was tidying up after Sunday school; strolling arm-in-arm across the meadows or having supper together at the rectory. Reverend and Mrs Linley still invited and welcomed her, but it wasn't the same without Gilbert. She found herself making excuses and declining their invitations. Being there in the rectory with the happily married old couple reminded Amy too sharply of what might have been, if only Gilbert had returned her love.

At this special time of year, with the church and town decked for Christmastide, Amy felt Gilbert's absence especially keenly. She wistfully recalled all the happy times they'd shared, and dwelled upon how they might have planned All Hallows' carollings, Christingle and Christmas morning music together.

After finishing at Jessup's, Amy set off along Abbotsgate to the greengrocer in search of small oranges for Sunday's Christingle. Having made her purchases, she was weaving through the busy street when Dan Ainsworth caught up with her.

'I'll walk you home. Market days are even more boisterous than usual leading up to Christmas.'

'I'd noticed.' She grimaced, skirting around a chestnut seller who was plainly the worse for wear and loudly heckling the pie-man on the opposite corner. 'Teddy told me you'd offered him free board and lodgings at the Mermaid. It's good of you, Dan. Thanks.'

'Edmund's a good lad and a hard worker, and it'd only be the room above the stable.' He shrugged. 'It might tide him over until you get settled somewhere. Have you been told when you have to leave Clockmakers?'

'Not until after Christmas; that's all we know as yet. Apparently the banker who lent Pa the money will send us a notice to quit, and that will have the date we need to leave the cottage.'

'It's a rum do and no mistake,' he said sympathetically. 'Have you seen anywhere likely? Ned and me and all of us, we've been keeping our eyes open for a place that might suit.'

'I know. Teddy told me. There's an empty cottage in the middle of Fisherman's Terrace. That's the best we've seen so far. Aunt Anne insisted we move in with her, but the schoolhouse is so tiny that it'd be cramped for two people, and we'd be five. Until Pa finds another job, we won't know how much rent we can afford to pay. But he's quite determined that we get settled in a new home long before we get turned out from Clockmakers. He couldn't bear the shame of our belongings being carted from the cottage and put out into the lane.'

'Your da's a proud man. His dignity's

already taken a battering from losing the *Jenet Rae*.'

'It's not being able to find any work and not being the family breadwinner anymore that's really eating away at him.' She frowned. 'He started looking as soon as he was up and about and able to walk, but he's not a young man. Jobs aren't easy to find.'

'Is it right he'll not go back to sea?'

She nodded. 'It surprised us, too. Pa's willing to try his hand at anything else — but he really doesn't want to have to go cap in hand to Alfred Paslew and beg for a job at the clay pits.'

'I don't blame him.' Dan paused. 'Which way are you going? Aren't you heading home?'

'I'm taking these oranges to All Hallows for Christingle.' She laughed out loud at his puzzled expression. 'You should come to church more often, Dan Ainsworth!'

'I'll be there on Christmas Day, just like every year,' he declared, walking with her. 'Amy, have you heard from

Fanny lately? Do you know what Theodore Buxton is up to these days?'

She gave him a wry glance. 'He's still in York. According to Fanny, he doesn't go away as often as he used to, and he's planning a very lavish festive session. They've taken on new servants, arranged dinners and parties, and employed a nurse to look after Fanny and take care of the baby when it comes. Why do you ask about Theo?'

'I've mentioned Sam Tristram, haven't I? Editor of the *Lancashire Clarion*? Told you about how he asked me to write up any local stories and send them in? Well, Sam's heard a rumour about a big railway shares swindle. Alfred Paslew was one of the investors.'

Amy's eyes widened. 'That's what Nick spoke about! Theo's selling shares for a railway that's never going to be built!'

'Happen Buxton's chickens are on their way home to roost,' he remarked with a grim smile. 'Sam Tristram's asked me to see what I can find out. I'm going up to Whiteladies to see if Paslew'll give me his comments for the *Clarion*. Mind you, he'll probably send me packing with a flea in my ear. His sort don't like being made a fool of, or want it written about for all to read.'

'Is that what it was? Foolishness?'

'Paslew's been conned, hasn't he?' Dan said with a shrug. 'Duped by a smooth-talking swindler. He's not the only one who was taken in by Buxton, though. A lot of other rich men invested, and there'll be some who'll be ruined.'

'What about Alfred Paslew? Will he be ruined?'

'Paslew's not that much of a fool,' snorted Dan derisively. 'No fear! He's the sort who always covers his back. He'll probably just cut his men's wages to make up for the losses.'

They passed through the lichgate and up to All Hallows. With a deep sigh, Amy pushed open the west door and, lighting the candle, walked into the dark church. 'I can't believe Christmas is almost here. I don't feel Christmassy at all.'

'Amy, do you remember me saying I'd keep asking you to marry me until you said yes? Well, I'll not ask you again. For there's one as stands between us, isn't there? Gilbert Paslew.' Dan paused. 'Do you write to each other?'

She shook her head. 'He corresponds with Teddy. Gilbert is helping him with his scholarship studies, as you know.'

'So Gilbert Paslew's gone, and you don't hear from him,' said Dan slowly. 'He might never come back, lass. Just because I'll not ask you again, doesn't mean my feelings have changed. They haven't, and this seems the right place to tell you so. All you need do is say the word, Amy.' He watched the candlelight flickering across her huge, sad eyes. 'I'll have you walking up this aisle so fast it'll make your head spin!'

*　*　*

The winter's first dusting of powdery snow helped the runners of Edmund's sled move easily across the coarse grass and fallen leaves in Friars Wood. He and Amy were gathering firewood, tying it into bundles and loading it upon the sled, while Vicky had gone in search of the perfect Yule log for Clockmakers Cottage.

'It's queer to think this'll be our last Christmas at Clockmakers, isn't it?' said Edmund, tying off another bundle. 'I hope Pa finds a job soon. He doesn't speak of it, but he goes to the boatyard every morning in case they need extra hands. Then he waits around at the quayside to be hired on for a day's work. But they always pick the young, stronger men.'

'That's awful — I had no idea!' cried Amy in dismay. 'Poor, poor Pa! After being a skipper for so many years, now he's having to . . . It must be so humiliating for him! I wish we could have spared him that, Teddy.'

Leaving Edmund to stack the last of the firewood onto the sled, she wandered through the trees into the dell and sank to her knees before St Agnes

Falls. A few minutes passed and she sensed, rather than heard, Edmund joining her.

'Wonder where we'll be this time next year?'

'You'll be away at school,' she replied lightly. 'Having passed the scholarship with flying colours!'

'I'm starting to really believe I will, you know,' he said seriously. 'Get a scholarship, that is, not the flying colours! Gilbert's shown me how to analyse and think properly. He's an excellent teacher. I never would have reached this standard without his help and guidance.'

'Is — is Gilbert well, Teddy?'

'Mmm, I think so. He always asks after you and the family.'

'We parted so abruptly. It wasn't even a proper goodbye. Will he be coming to Whiteladies Grange for Christmas?'

Edmund shook his head. 'He's staying with the family of one of his old tutors in Oxford. The Right Reverend someone-or-other. Gilbert's intending to offer himself as a candidate for Holy Orders.'

Amy smiled wistfully, touching her fingertips to the spring's cold, clear waters. 'The Dog Star showed Gilbert his rightful path after all!'

'What?' queried Edmund, mystified.

'Nothing,' she replied, rising and brushing down her skirts. 'Let's see if Vicky has found us our Yule log.'

Hauling their laden sled, the three presently emerged from Friars Wood a little way beyond the church, and were walking down Lane End towards the schoolhouse to leave Anne's share of the firewood.

'Aunt Anne must have company,' remarked Edmund when the schoolhouse came within sight. 'Company with a fine carriage, no less.'

'That's the Paslew carriage! We'd better wait a bit, Teddy. We don't want to barge in,' Amy said, slowing her step. 'Let's go along the riverbank and find some intact seed heads for the Christmas table.'

Edmund stowed the sled just inside the little north gate of All Hallows and they set off along Lane End. A stout man carrying a small black bag was hammering on the door of the brick house nearest the river.

'I think that's Meggie Huxley's dad,' muttered Edmund, who'd admired Meggie Huxley from afar for some considerable while. 'Doesn't look very pleased, does he?'

'Judging from the bag, he must be the landlord collecting his rents,' observed Amy, glancing at the house's grimy windows. 'I don't think he'll have much luck there — it looks empty.'

They'd no sooner passed Martin Huxley when he turned around and called out after them. 'Miss! Do you know owt about the folk who live here? A couple, with three or four bairns. Have you seen 'em today?'

'I'm sorry, I don't know of the family,' replied Amy, looking back at the house once more as she and the others contin-ued onto the riverbank.

When they returned a short while later with a basketful of silvery teasel, feathery gypsy grass and velvety brown bulrush, the landlord was still working his way along Lane End collecting rents.

'Aye, the house *is* empty, miss,' was Huxley's response to Amy's enquiry. 'I've let myself inside and there's not so much as a stick or a thread. Done a flit, they have. Cleared the place out and gone off owing their rent money!'

Upon finding out how much the rent was, Amy asked if she might view the house, and Huxley handed over the key. 'By the time you've looked around, I'll be across the road collecting. You can fetch the key to me there. Don't be long making your mind up about t'house — I need to get a tenant right away. I can't afford to lose another week's rent money.'

The three Macfarlenes stood outside in the lane, looking up at the brick house for a few minutes before unlocking the door and going inside.

'Everything needs a thorough scrubbing, but that's easily remedied,' Amy commented, going through the three downstairs rooms. 'Mr Huxley must be a decent landlord, for the house seems in sound repair.'

'Come and have a look up here!' called Edmund, adding when Amy and Vicky climbed the narrow stair, 'The windows on that side overlook the church, and from here you can see for miles across Friars Wood to the hills.'

'There's the big house!' exclaimed Vicky, pointing to the slate roofs and stone chimneys of Whiteladies Grange. 'That's where Amy and I went when I fell out of the tree!'

'With work, the garden could be nice,' Amy said, looking down. 'Plenty of room for a vegetable patch, and the pear tree in the corner is strong enough for Vicky's swing.'

'Of all the houses we've seen, this is the best,' agreed Edmund. 'It's very near the school, too.'

'Are we going to live here?' Vicky's bright blue eyes darted excitedly from Edmund to Amy. 'Are we?'

'We'll have to see what Pa thinks,' Amy said with a smile, tugging Vicky's plaits as they went downstairs. 'I'll return Mr Huxley's key, and then we'll take Aunt Anne her firewood.'

Vicky burst into the schoolhouse and told Anne all about the empty house at Lane End long before Amy and Edmund had put away the firewood and taken off their coats. 'I didn't know the family who lived there very well,' remarked Anne, setting down a tray of tea, hot buttered toast and honey before her nephew and nieces. 'They hadn't been in Monks Quay for very long, and weren't church-goers. They didn't send their children to school, either, which did not make me well-disposed toward them. However, I had no inkling they were the sort who would sneak away without paying their debts.'

'Providing Pa approves, I think we should take it,' said Amy, swirling honey onto her toast. 'The rent is reasonable and the house seems solid.'

'I remember those houses at Lane

End being built when your mother and I were young. They were much admired.' Anne joined them at the table. 'You've only just missed Eleanor Paslew. She came visiting this afternoon and we had such a nice conversation, wandering down memory lane for much of the time. Eleanor has invited me to Whiteladies Grange for tea — I shall look forward to that — and she brought me a box of sugared almonds. Even after so many years, she remembered that was my favourite. I've put the box away — we'll open it after Christmas dinner.'

'Mrs Paslew always spoke very fondly of you when I was at Whiteladies,' said Amy. 'Did you and she have a falling out or something?'

'No. Never so much as a cross word passed between us. As we grew up, I suppose our lives went in different directions, and without ever meaning to, we simply drifted apart. Eleanor had it in a nutshell this afternoon when she remarked upon how very easy it is to lose touch with those you care about and not even notice the years rushing by.' It seemed to Amy that her aunt's stern gaze was inexplicably fixed upon her. 'If reunions are delayed, all too soon it becomes too late, and the parting is forever.'

* * *

Amy looked up from her sewing when Ramsay came home after spending another day searching for work, and knew from her father's face that he had not been successful. She saw his grimace of pain as he sat down, easing his right leg out straight and propping his stick against the table. He drank the hot, sweet tea she put before him without uttering a word.

'Pa, are you certain about coming ashore?' she ventured. 'You love the sea, and with all your experience, any master would be glad to have you sign on.'

'It's high time I came ashore and looked after my family,' he replied wearily. 'Should've done it years ago. That truth hit me hard when the *Jenet Rae* was getting pulled by the ebb up toward the Judas Rocks. I kept thinking about the three of you being left to fend for yourselves, and me not being around to watch you grow up, or see Fanny's babe when it comes. We could've all drowned that night, Amy. Every last man of us. Probably would've, but for Ned sending out the torches. So you see, lass, my mind's made up. I don't care what I do — not even if it's at Paslew's clay pits, although that would be a bitter pill to swallow. But as long as it's honest work, and we're all still together — '

'Pa!' Vicky barrelled into the cottage after helping Edmund stack the firewood. 'We've found a new house!'

While Ramsay had another cup of tea, they told him about Lane End. 'I know that house, and it's a good 'un.' He drained his tea and got awkwardly to his feet. 'I'll go and see Mr Huxley right away and get my name on the rent book. We'll move in on Boxing Day. I just hope we're in time and nobody else has snapped it up.'

Nobody had. Amy and the others went into Monks Quay with Ramsay, and they walked back to Clockmakers in good spirits with a month's rent paid and the rent book and keys of Lane End safely in their possession. They were about five minutes from the cottage when a figure appeared from the darkness.

'Ah! There you all are!' Dan greeted them. 'I've been knocking at your door. This letter came with tonight's coach. It's not Fanny's handwriting, but I thought it might be important.'

He caught Amy's eye as Ramsay thanked him and took the thick letter. When the others moved on towards Clockmakers, she hung back to speak to him.

'What is it, Dan?'

'That letter might be important — it looks like it's travelled a long way. But bringing it out here was an excuse to see you,' he confessed shamelessly. 'We're having a Christmas dance at the

Mermaid this market night. Will you come with me? All the money goes to the parish fund so if you refuse, you'll be doing needy folk out of their pennies.'

'Dan, I still love Gilbert,' Amy murmured frankly. 'I always shall.'

'Fair enough. But what's the harm in two old friends spending an evening together?' he persisted brightly. 'It *is* Christmas!'

'You're hopeless.'

'I'm also a very good dancer, so I'm told. You can't shut yourself away forever. Will you come?'

She reflected a moment before nodding. 'I'd like to go dancing with you.'

'Good lass!' He looked sorely tempted to kiss her, but didn't. 'I knew you wouldn't let me end up a wallflower!'

Hurrying along the rough sandy track, she followed the family into Clockmakers Cottage. Edmund had lit the lamp and Pa was breaking the seal on the bulky letter. 'It's money!' he exclaimed, studying the half-dozen lines scrawled on the thick paper. 'From Rory!'

'It's his writing,' said Edmund, peering over his father's shoulder. 'But it's signed 'Robbie'.'

'Robbie was the pet name your ma and I gave Rory when he was a bairn, long before any of you came along,' answered Ramsay, adding solemnly, 'Seems he's had need to change his name.'

'He's living in Argentina!' read Amy, scarcely able to believe her eyes. 'He's safe and doing well. He must be! That's an awful lot of money!'

'It is, that.' Ramsay clumsily bundled it and the letter together, jamming them behind Ma's tea caddy on the dresser. 'And I'll crawl on my hands and knees and beg Alfred Paslew for a job in his clay pits before I'll touch a penny piece of it! Rory's my lad and I'm thankful he's still alive and safe. But sure as night follows day, that money's dishonestly come by, and Lord alone knows how much bloodshed might be behind it!'

* * *

Rory's letter was still propped behind the tea caddy on Boxing Day morning when Amy rose early to make ready for the move to Lane End. She couldn't help but wonder what her brother had done after fleeing Carteret Square, and how he came to prosper so very far away in South America. Placing the letter in Pa's satchel, along with the rest of the family papers and valuables, she set to clearing the dresser, cupboards and pantry and packing the contents into tea chests.

She, Vicky and Aunt Anne had spent the days before Christmas scrubbing and scouring at Lane End so that the new house would be clean and ready. Dan brought the wagon up to Clockmakers, and after numerous trips back and forth, on foot as well as wheels, by nightfall the Macfarlenes were sitting down to their first meal at Lane End.

The medieval bells of All Hallows rang out the old year and rung in the new, and the weeks began slipping by. Everything went on much as before. Vicky went to school, Ramsay persevered with his search for regular work, Edmund studied constantly and became increasingly nervous as his scholarship examinations approached, and Amy did all she could to make their new home a comfortable and happy one. She'd been working late at Jessup's, and upon stepping out into the windswept night was inexorably drawn down to the deserted shore.

Standing on the damp sand, she breathed deeply, absorbing the power and the wildness; feeling the roar and crash of the tide sweeping up from the night, billowing and breaking in wavelets just inches from her feet. Until that very moment, Amy had not realised how she pined for the sounds of the sea, which were constant at Clockmakers Cottage regardless of the tide, or how sorely she missed the lonely cry of the gulls and the sharp, fresh salty air.

Turning from the water's edge, her gaze drifted along the strand to Clockmakers. It stood alone in the darkness, the pale moonshine reflecting on its blank windows. She was dismayed to see the cottage looking desolate and forlorn. It was for sale now, and she pondered who might buy her old home, and what sort of family would make it their own. Quickening her pace, she left the shore and began the long walk back into Monks Quay.

Despite the lateness of the hour, a light was showing at the schoolhouse, and Amy knocked at Aunt Anne's door.

'I saw you were still up. I've brought you this.' She held out a book of poetry. 'Mr Jessup bought a chest of second-hand books from Lancaster and I've been sorting them for the shelves. This is for you.'

'William Cowper! How wonderful!' exclaimed Anne, glancing at the pages. 'What a handsome volume!'

'I mentioned how much you admired Cowper, and Mr Jessup said you were most welcome to have it.'

'Wasn't that kind of him! And you too, my dear,' said Anne with a smile. 'I'm pleased Lane End has turned out well for you all. For me, too. It's lovely having you nearby.'

Impulsively, Amy hugged her aunt's bony shoulders. She was keenly aware how attached Anne was to Clockmakers Cottage, and how deeply saddened she must be by its loss from the family.

'I'm so sorry, Aunt.'

'There, now. It's all right.' She held Amy at arm's length. 'You're looking tired and far too thin. Continue like this, and Gilbert won't recognise you when he returns!'

Amy was resigned. 'There's nothing for him in Monks Quay, Aunt. He said that. He won't come back.'

'Won't he?' Anne tilted her head. 'If and when he does return, don't waste any time in building your bridges!'

* * *

Everyone was abed when Amy let herself in at Lane End. Aunt Anne had been right about one thing — she was tired. Without bothering to heat up her share of the cobbler she'd made for the

310

family's supper, she took the lamp to the table, washed her hands and picked up her sewing. There wasn't much of this week's batch left to do. She'd press the work in the morning and take the basket over to Whiteladies before going on to Jessup's.

Mrs Paslew was a generous employer, and Amy's wages from the weekly basket of needlework, together with making the curtains for the main downstairs rooms at Whiteladies, were a godsend. Although Pa did odd jobs around the town, the family was struggling without a man's regular wage. But for Amy's contribution, they wouldn't be able to make ends meet.

Sleet was driving down from the distant hills and cutting across the stubbly fields when Amy scurried from Lane End next morning, taking a short cut through Friars Wood to Whiteladies Grange. Her head was bowed against the weather and both of her arms were wrapped about the sewing basket as she ran the last few yards across the cobbles of the turning circle towards the rear door, realising too late that Alfred Paslew had been watching her approach from the coach-house and was stepping out to block her progress.

'Miss Macfarlene.' His voice was quiet and brusque. 'I owe you an apology. Overdue, I'm afraid. I acted in haste. Unwisely so, I now believe. That's all. You may continue about your business. Good morning to you.' With that, he marched back into the coach-house.

Astonished, Amy sped the remaining yards across the cobbles to the kitchen. She was still mulling over the unexpected encounter with Mr Paslew on her way down Lane End to Jessup's when Ned and her father passed in a great hurry.

'We can't stop!' called Ramsay breathlessly. 'Ned's just come and tipped me the word that a bloke at the boatyard has taken bad. If I get along there quick, I may get his job!'

'If it's the consumption, he'll not be needing it yet awhile. Maybe not ever,' panted Ned grimly. 'And it sounded like the consumption to me.'

'Keep your fingers crossed, lass — this'd be right up my street!'

★ ★ ★

Choir practice wasn't the same without Gilbert leading it. Amy attended regularly nonetheless, and when she arrived home after that evening's session and there was no sign of Pa, she hoped it was because he'd been taken on at the boatyard. Sure enough, when he came in just as the meal was put upon the table, Ramsay didn't need to say a word — it was written plain across his face.

'I can turn my hand to most things, when it comes to boats — I've had to over the years,' he declared, handing Amy a flask of local oak cider. 'Mull that for us, lass, and fetch your Aunt Anne to join us. We'll have a cup — even you, Vicky, with plenty of water — to celebrate me having a proper job again!'

As Amy mixed honey and cloves into the oak cider, added a cinnamon stick and gently warmed the golden concoction, the family's talk around the table was the liveliest she'd heard in many a month. It was such a blessing to see Pa his old self again. A great burden had been removed from his shoulders, Amy knew. Although she didn't give them voice, her thoughts strayed to the man who had been taken so poorly, and to those who depended upon him.

'By, that smells grand!' said Ramsay with a big smile when she brought the mulled cider to the table. 'I want us to raise our cups not only to celebrate my new job, but to toast Ted, who has his examinations coming up. Here's to you, my boy!' He reached across the table to slap his son's shoulder. 'You're going to do us all proud.'

* * *

When the day came for Edmund to go up to Preston and sit his scholarship examination, Amy was struck by how very young and lost he looked. She slipped her arm through his as they waited at the Mermaid Inn for the coach.

'Are you sure you'll have enough to read on the journey?' she asked, trying to make him smile and nodding to the huge bag of books at his feet. It worked — nearly.

'There *are* a lot! I'm afraid I'll forget something and need to look it up again before I go in to the examination room.'

'I'm sure you won't need them,' Amy reassured him. 'But it's sensible to have them with you, just in case.'

Edmund nodded vigorously. 'That's what Gilbert said. I'm glad he's coming up from Oxford to meet me there. We're going to revise all this evening, and first thing tomorrow before the examination begins.'

Amy bit back questions she would've liked to ask about Gilbert. She tried not to speak of him too often. It didn't help. 'Don't worry, Teddy. You know your subjects and you'll pass.'

'I have to, Amy. I just *have* to!' His

smooth face creased into an anxious frown. 'Pa has all his hopes pinned on me — I couldn't bear to let him down!'

The coach duly departed and Amy cheerily waved Edmund out of sight, scarcely aware Dan had come to stand at her side.

'He'll do fine. Edmund's got a grand future ahead of him.'

'He deserves it. I've never known anyone work so hard.'

'Happen he gets that from his big sister!' said Dan with a grin as he shook a newspaper from his coat pocket. 'The *Clarion* came with the coach. The story about the railway shares swindle has broken.'

Amy took the paper, folded it open at a long article, and immediately saw Dan's name in bold print next to the editor's. 'My goodness, Dan! Congratulations!'

'I didn't write all of it, just contributed,' he said, pleased at her enthusiastic reaction. 'Paslew wouldn't speak to me, but the editor gave me a few leads, and I tracked down this man Spofforth. He had plenty to say! He's got a flax mill down over at Croskirk. At least, he did have. Theodore Buxton fleeced him good and proper. Spofforth lost the lot.'

'The newspaper doesn't mention Theo by name.'

'The editor has to be careful about naming names. It's early days yet.'

'If only Fanny and Nick weren't part of Theo's household. It's wrong they have to face the consequences of his trouble!'

'They're innocent and have nothing to fear,' Dan said, walking with her to Jessup's. 'Which is more than can be said for Theodore Buxton. His worst nightmare is about to come true!'

* * *

When Edmund got back to Monks Quay later that week, he stretched out in the comfortable fireside chair and folded his arms across his chest. 'I can't believe it's over. All those books. All those months and months of reading them and thinking about them. Of course, if I pass and am offered a place at school, the *real* studying will be only just beginning!'

'That's true!' said Amy with a smile as she took out her crochet. She was working the sleeve of a jacket to match the bonnet and shawl she'd already made for Fanny's baby. 'Ever since I saw that piece in the Clarion, I haven't stopped thinking about Fanny. It can't be very long before her time, Teddy.'

'Will Theo go to gaol?'

'I don't know what'll happen. Although Dan explained it to me as best he could, I still don't quite understand how Theo cheated all those people out of their money.'

'Gilbert said an odd thing,' mused Edmund after they'd fallen silent for a while. 'He always does ask about you in his letters, but when I saw him in Preston, he asked me if you and Dan were married! He and his father are reconciled, by the way. He said his father has finally accepted there are worse things than having a son who's a clergyman — although probably not many!'

Amy tensed. The notion of Gilbert believing she was married to Dan Ainsworth was peculiarly disconcerting, and the uneasiness stayed with her long after Edmund had mentioned it.

The next morning, as she was in the kitchen cutting bread and cheese for her father's carry-out, she was half-listening to him expounding to her about some tricky aspect of caulking as he got ready for work.

'So we got that sorted out, and I was just knocking off when Seth Pickering — he has the ships' chandlers at the boatyard; I've known him years — comes across and says he has to go out for a couple of hours, and will I look after the shop for him? So I did, and thoroughly enjoyed it! It's a tidy little business Seth's got there. When he got back, he said he'd put a few hours' work my way whenever he needed to go out. It saves shutting the shop. He's on his own, y'see. He was telling me he's had a few assistants in the past, but they always ended up with their fingers in the till, so he manages without 'em now.' Taking his carry-out and wrapping his muffler about his neck, he started out of the kitchen door. 'Oh, summat else Seth was telling me — Clockmakers Cottage is sold. He don't know who to. Nobody local, anyhow.'

Amy's spirits sank. That the cottage would one day be sold had been inevitable, but its occurring now only deepened a despair that refused to lift as the day wore on. It was mid-afternoon, and she was in Jessup's wrapping a bottle of Indian Ink, when Teddy burst into the stationer's.

'Amy — you'd better come!'

Brother and sister sped along Abbotsgate, with Edmund hurriedly explaining he'd been working in the stables as usual when the coach had arrived.

'In here!' He held open the front door of the Mermaid Inn and Amy hurried inside. Fanny was sitting straight-backed before the parlour fire, a pot of tea on the table beside her and her bags, boxes and the Shawcross walnut corner clock stacked on the floor at her feet.

'Theo has deserted me, Amy,' she declared, raising furious eyes to her sister. 'I've come home!'

* * *

Fanny's daughter was born on the day the first wild daffodils were flowering in Friars Wood. Amy crept upstairs into the room where Grace was sleeping contentedly in her mother's arms, and sat beside Fanny's bed.

'She's beautiful, Fan! If only Ma were here to see you both.'

'I've been thinking about Ma, too,' said Fanny with a smile. 'She would have loved being a grandma. For his part, Pa is taking his new responsibilities very seriously — I understand it's drinks all round at the Mermaid!'

Amy laughed. 'He's thrilled to bits.'

'Do you think Pa is serious about the ships' chandlers, Amy? For weeks now, it's been a real bee in his bonnet.'

Fanny was right — their father was much taken with the prospect of buying into the thriving little shop. 'I think Pa will go into partnership with Seth Pickering one day. It would make good sense for both of them,' said Amy. 'However, he can't afford it until he sells the *Jenet Rae*, and he's determined to fix her up first, so he can get a good price.'

'It seems everything comes down to profit, doesn't it?' reflected Fanny, smoothing a flaxen curl from Grace's forehead. 'Recently, I've questioned whether Theo ever loved me at all.'

'He adored you, Fanny — I heard him telling Nick so,' replied Amy at once. 'There isn't any doubt Theo loves you.'

'Isn't there?' her sister queried evenly. 'I knew Theo inherited the house at Carteret Square from his maternal grandfather. But just before he ran away to avoid being arrested as a common criminal, I discovered Carteret Square was left to Theo in trust! It became his only upon marriage.'

'Oh, Fan!' cried Amy. 'You can't think — '

'I can, Amy. And I do,' she replied briskly. 'Theo left me in the final weeks of my confinement, without any thought for me or his unborn child. Heaven knows what I would've done without Nicholas to stay with me in York and manage the shameful catastrophe Theo left behind!'

'Nick's a good man,' Amy said quietly. 'He cares deeply for you and Grace.'

'I know he does, and I care deeply for him.' She tenderly kissed Grace's downy cheek. 'I've had ample time and reason to repent marrying the wrong brother!'

* * *

On the day Edmund received the results of his scholarship examination, the coach from York brought Nicholas Buxton to Monks Quay. Deciding to leave Fanny and Nick to talk privately, Amy and Edmund took Vicky and Grace out into the warm sunshine of the spring afternoon. Edmund's curiosity about Theo's criminal activities was as nothing compared to his euphoria at gaining a scholarship. He'd read the letter at least eight times, to Amy's certain knowledge!

'We've a lot to do to get you ready to go, Teddy,' she remarked practically. 'Easter isn't so far off, and the term starts straight afterwards.'

'I'm really excited.' He beamed. 'But I'm nervous, too! By the time they were my age, Gilbert and Nicholas had already been away at school for years and years. I'm not really looking forward to living in lodgings with total strangers, either.'

'I'm sure the school wouldn't recommend this establishment if it were not clean and respectable,' replied Amy, consulting the letter again. 'Oh, Teddy — A 'Pass with Distinction'! We're all so very proud of you!'

Late into that night, Amy and Fanny sat up sipping hot cocoa, talking quietly and sharing confidences just as they had done so many times in their long room under the eaves at Clockmakers Cottage. Fanny's fair ringlets gleamed in the soft light as she cradled Grace in her arms; and despite all the recent troubles, Amy had never seen her elder sister more composed.

'Nicholas brought me a letter and money from Theo. He's in India,' she explained simply. 'Apparently, when he left me in York, Theo only narrowly avoided arrest. Investors lost a fortune; my husband made one. He's a wealthy man again now, and wants Grace and me to sail with Nicholas to India. Theo wishes us all to make a fresh start there.'

'In India?' echoed Amy in consternation. 'When is Nick sailing?'

'The week after next.'

'At least it gives you a little time to make up your mind.'

'I don't need any time,' Fanny answered, drawing the soft wool of the crocheted shawl closer about her daughter. 'I'd already reached a decision concerning my marriage long before Nicholas brought Theo's letter. Grace and I are settled here in Monks Quay. I'm not inclined to leave again.'

'If that's what you truly want — I'm so glad, Fan!'

'Well, honestly, imagine what that blazing sun would do to my complexion!' she returned crisply. 'I'd be constantly worried lest my fair hair started looking horsey, too.'

Amy laughed. 'You don't change, Fanny!'

'I do, Amy. And I have,' she murmured seriously. 'For the better, I think.'

'What of Nick? Will he stay out in India?'

'Nicholas loves his brother, Amy. Nothing will ever change that. He wants to do the honourable thing and see Theo face to face. That's very important to him. But no, he won't stay in India.' Fanny met Amy's gaze steadily. 'Nicholas wishes to make his home and future here in Monks Quay.'

★ ★ ★

Nicholas Buxton accompanied the Macfarlenes to All Hallows on Sunday morning, pausing to shake hands and pay his respects to the Paslews as he passed by their family pew. Fanny had been worried about taking Grace to church for the first time, lest she become agitated amongst so many strangers and start to cry. Amy was certain there'd been no need for Fanny's concern, for even from her seat at the front of the choir stalls she could see that her little niece was wide awake and perfectly content, not so much as batting an eye when the organ groaned noisily into life and Aunt Anne struck the opening chords of the first hymn.

The deep richness of an achingly familiar tenor voice flooded Amy's senses when the singing began. She couldn't glance around, but as the service unfolded, she was increasingly aware of Gilbert's presence just a yard or so behind her. She heard not a word of Reverend Linley's sermon until he actually mentioned Gilbert by name, and her attention riveted upon the elderly man.

' . . . has been ordained in Holy Orders, and Monks Quay is to be his first curacy.

I feel doubly blessed,' William Linley was saying genially. 'Not only do I at long last have a curate to assist me, but this curate is my own dear nephew! I'm sure we're both eagerly anticipating working together and serving our parishioners. Indeed, next week, Gilbert will be performing the christening of little Grace, who is with us this morning — and unlike some other members of the congregation, is still awake! Now, for our final hymn . . . '

As was the custom, the choir remained seated while the congregation filed out. When All Hallows was almost empty and the choir rising, Amy was aware of Gilbert moving to her side. Her intention of slipping away without seeing him was dashed.

'Amy?'

Awkwardly, she half-turned, but did not raise her eyes, fumbling instead with her music.

'Amy,' he went on softly, 'may I walk with you?'

An excuse — any excuse — was on

the tip of her tongue. She didn't want to walk with him or be with him or speak to him! It would open old wounds and hurt too much. Already, the longing for him she had striven so hard to bury was slicing through her as keenly as upon that fateful night when they'd parted.

Of a sudden, she realised everyone else had gone from All Hallows. She and Gilbert were alone. The quietness drummed unbearably inside her ears. The dancing shafts of brilliant sunlight and potent fragrance of spring flowers were making her dizzy, and the white-washed walls and stone floor of the ancient church swam before her eyes. She desperately wanted to escape this intimacy and be out in the cool, reviving fresh air; to have these awful first moments over and done with. They could not be evaded, however. For Gilbert was curate at All Hallows now, and Amy would have to become accustomed to being in his presence.

Taking a deep breath, she inclined her head and moved from the choir stalls, walking slightly ahead of Gilbert from the church. Once outside, he fell into step beside her, and they started across the meadows from All Hallows down toward the sea, just as they'd done upon so many other Sundays.

'I . . . I'd imagined you would be married to Dan Ainsworth,' he said hesitantly. 'Then I found it wasn't so. Not yet, at least. Do you and he have intentions, Amy?'

'No, we do not!' she retorted agitatedly, her eyes fixed upon the horizon as they walked. 'Dan and I are old friends, but we certainly aren't lovers!'

'Are you not?' he challenged quietly. 'The night I came to Clockmakers Cottage to tell you I was going to Oxford and beg you to wait for me, he was with you! I heard the way he spoke to you, Amy. Saw how he looked at you! When I reached for you, you shrank away,' he continued harshly. 'What was I supposed to think? You couldn't bear to let me touch you!'

Shaking her head in disbelief, Amy

rounded on him, her eyes blazing. 'If only you knew . . . '

Gilbert caught his breath, gazing down at her and searching the depths of her eyes. And suddenly, he *did* know. 'Amy — ' He spoke her name urgently, pulling her to him. ' — I have loved you for . . . I never want to lose you again!'

'You couldn't,' she whispered brokenly. 'I've always been yours.'

Presently, they continued strolling along the shore. 'There's something I should tell you,' Gilbert said simply. 'When I heard Clockmakers Cottage was for sale, I bought it . . . in the hope you'd consider becoming my wife and live there with me.'

They had reached the cottage gate, and his arms encircled Amy's slender waist. 'Will you?' He smiled between kisses. 'Has that Dog Star of yours led me on a true course?'

Breathlessly, Amy laughed up into his grey eyes. 'Gilbert . . . the Dog Star has brought us *both* safely home!'

We do hope that you have enjoyed reading this large print book.

Did you know that all of our titles are available for purchase?

We publish a wide range of high quality large print books including:
Romances, Mysteries, Classics General Fiction Non Fiction and Westerns

Special interest titles available in large print are:
The Little Oxford Dictionary Music Book, Song Book Hymn Book, Service Book

Also available from us courtesy of Oxford University Press:
Young Readers' Dictionary (large print edition) Young Readers' Thesaurus (large print edition)

For further information or a free brochure, please contact us at:
Ulverscroft Large Print Books Ltd., The Green, Bradgate Road, Anstey, Leicester, LE7 7FU, England. Tel: (00 44) 0116 236 4325 **Fax:** (00 44) 0116 234 0205

*Other titles in the
Linford Romance Library:*

CHRISTMAS REVELATIONS

Jill Barry

Reluctant 1920s debutante Annabel prefers horses to suitors. When she tumbles into the path of Lawrence, Lord Lassiter, she's annoyed that this attractive man is the despised thirteenth guest joining her family for Christmas — for he has been involved in a recent scandal, and only he and his faithful valet, Norman Bassett, know the truth behind the gossip. Meanwhile, as Lawrence tries to charm Annabel, Norman has a surprise encounter with a figure from his past — one who has been keeping a secret from him for years . . .

WHERE THE HEART LIES

Sheila Spencer-Smith

Amy sets off to join her wildlife photographer boyfriend Mark on the Isles of Scilly, accompanied by her sister's dog Rufus, who she is dropping off with her sister's parents-in-law, Jim and Maria, at Penmarrow Caravan Site. But when she arrives, the park is deserted — except for the handsome Callum Savernack, who doesn't appear happy to have her there. When it emerges that Jim and Maria are temporarily unable to return to Penmarrow, Amy finds herself torn between her responsibilities to Mark, to Rufus — and to Callum . . .

THE SHADOW IN THE DARK

Susan Udy

Attempting to escape the scandal that has engulfed her, Daisy Lewis leaves home and heads for the Cornish town of Pencarrow, still as beautiful as she remembers from her childhood holidays. But news spreads like wildfire in the small, tightly knit community, and soon she must deal with a blackmailer who recognises her from her previous life. Even worse, she suspects it could be one of the two handsome men who are keen to romance her. Is there anyone Daisy can trust — and will her secret be exposed yet again?

ENCHANTMENT IN MOROCCO

Madeleine McDonald

Stranded in Morocco, Emily Ryan accepts a job offer from a stranger. Entranced by her new life in the sleepy coastal village of Taghar, she struggles to resist widower Rafi Hassan's charm — but also clashes with his autocratic ways and respect for tradition. As she attempts to persuade him to allow his teenage daughter Nour more freedom, Emily refuses to acknowledge her own errors of judgement. As the seasons turn and the olives ripen, Emily dares to dream of winning Rafi's heart — until danger threatens from an unexpected quarter . . .

NO TIME FOR SECOND BEST

Jo Bartlett

When Ellie Chapman finds out that she's inherited her Great-aunt Hilary's farm on the beautiful Kentish coast, and is then made redundant from her office job, it looks like life has handed her the new start she's been craving. But there are choppy waters ahead, from difficulties with her ex-fiancé, to the unexpectedly dilapidated state of the farm, to a menagerie with a poorly donkey and a wayward sheep. Love is waiting in the wings for both Ellie and her mum, however, as well as some exciting new opportunities . . .

A TEMPORARY ARRANGEMENT

Pamela Fudge

Roz, a career-minded HR worker, and Sam, a successful country and western singer, are good friends. *Just good friends* — who have been engaged to each other for six years . . . Their sham attachment began by mutual agreement: a way of keeping the media from nosing into Sam's private life, and stopping Roz's Great-Aunt Ellen fretting about her great-niece's single state. And it's worked like a dream — until now. Because Roz wants to end the pretence. But Sam seems oddly reluctant to do so . . .